Happily Ever After Rescue Team

HAPPILY EVER AFTER RESCUE TEAM

SAM HAY

illustrated by
GENEVIEVE KOTE

Feiwel and Friends

New York

A Feiwel and Friends Book
An imprint of Macmillan Publishing Group, LLC
120 Broadway, New York, NY 10271 • mackids.com

Our books may be purchased in bulk for promotional, educational,
or business use. Please contact your local bookseller or the Macmillan
Corporate and Premium Sales Department at (800) 221-7945 ext. 5442
or by email at MacmillanSpecialMarkets@macmillan.com.

Library of Congress Cataloging-in-Publication Data

Names: Hay, Sam, author. | Kote, Genevieve, illustrator.
Title: Happily ever after rescue team / Sam Hay ; illustrated by
 Genevieve Kote.
Description: First edition. | New York : Feiwel and Friends, 2022. |
 Series: Agents of H.E.A.R.T. ; 1 | Summary: "A young girl's wish to help
 out in her family's seaside café gets out of hand when she accidentally
 summons a rescue squad of fairy-tale princesses." —Provided by publisher.
Identifiers: LCCN 2021026393 | ISBN 9781250798299 (hardcover) |
 ISBN 9781250798305 (trade paperback)
Subjects: CYAC: Magic—Fiction. | Princesses—Fiction. | Fairy tales—
 Fiction. | Family-owned business enterprises—Fiction.
Classification: LCC PZ7.H31387385 Hap 2022 | DDC [Fic]—dc23
LC record available at https://lccn.loc.gov/2021026393

First edition, 2022
Book design by Liz Dresner
Feiwel and Friends logo designed by Filomena Tuosto
Printed in the United States of America by LSC Communications,
Harrisonburg, Virginia

ISBN 978-1-250-79829-9 (hardcover)
1   3   5   7   9   10   8   6   4   2

ISBN 978-1-250-79830-5 (paperback)
1   3   5   7   9   10   8   6   4   2

For my daughter, Alice, the inspiration for Evie

CHAPTER 1

Every second counted. Which was why Evie was watching her stepmom, Hannah, like a hawk. Once Hannah finished taking the order from the old couple at table nine and headed to the kitchen to fetch their lunch, Evie estimated she'd have around two minutes—just 120 seconds—before her stepmom would be back. *Which should give me just enough time*, she thought, *to dash behind the counter and make the two Blueberry Blaster Slushie drinks for*

the teenagers at table two, which Hannah has forgotten to do!

The moment Evie had heard the teenagers order their drinks, she'd been itching to go make them. Evie LOVED making slushies. Especially Blueberry Blaster Slushies. There was something so satisfying about piling the fruit and ice into the blender and hitting the max power button so the machine whizzed and crunched and created the most delicious purple frothy drink ever! But her stepmom wasn't wild about letting Evie help out in the family's diner. *Mostly because I spill stuff,* Evie thought. *But I've been practicing and today I'm Wonder Waitress! The slickest smoothie-making superhero in the world! And I'm going to show Hannah just how awesome I am.*

Hannah had finished writing on her order pad now and was telling the old couple she would be back with their soup shortly.

Okay, begin countdown . . . Evie told herself . . . *Ten, nine, eight, seven . . .* Evie kept her eyes glued to Hannah as her stepmom turned and walked toward the kitchen, stopping to collect some dirty plates on her way.

Evie smiled as Hannah passed the diner counter, where she was supposed to be folding napkins. *Three, two, one . . . YES! She's out of sight! Go, Evie! Go!* She zipped around the back of the counter, grabbed the blueberry box, reached for the watermelon chunks, and dumped the lot into the blender. *Now for the crunchy bit!* She pulled open the refrigerator and found a bag of ice chips, keeping her eye on the diner clock. *Forty-five seconds gone. Quick, Evie! You mustn't let Hannah see you, not until you've safely delivered the slushies to the customers.*

 ## EVIE BROWN'S BLUEBERRY BLASTER SLUSHIE RECIPE

You will need:

- 2 cups of frozen blueberries
- 1 cup of watermelon chunks

- 1 tablespoon of lime or lemon juice

- ½ cup of sugar

- 2 cups of ice chips

Method:

- Blend together the fruit, sugar, and lemon/lime juice.

- Add the ice chips and blend. Or put the chips in a sandwich bag and bash with a rolling pin to crush.

- Empty everything into a jug, stir well, and serve.

- Decorate glasses with slices of lime and tiny umbrellas!

Evie hit the button on the blender and turned up the dial to max power. While it was whizzing and crunching, she found two smoothie glasses and some slices of lime to decorate the drinks with, as well as two tiny parasols. Evie loved the little umbrellas. *They look like they've been left behind by forgetful fairies*, she thought. Then—"Done!" Evie said, flicking off the blender and pouring out the thick, purple liquid. She added the decorations, then stood back to admire her work. *Yay! Two super exciting, taste-bud tingling slushie sensations for the teenagers at table two.* She placed the drinks on a tray, picked it up, and walked proudly around the counter to deliver them. *Wow!* she thought, checking the clock. *Finished with twenty seconds to spare. I really am Wonder Waitress, the only superhero who can balance a tray of Blueberry Blaster Slushies on one hand without dropping a—*

SMASH!

Everyone in the café turned to stare as the glasses crashed onto the tiles.

Uh-oh! Maybe I shouldn't have tried the one-handed tray trick. Evie shut her eyes and crossed her fingers and wished extra hard that when she opened them again either *she* would have vanished, or all

the customers would have gone. She opened one eye. *Nope, that didn't work.* She bit her lip and tried to smile as everyone stared at her, mouths open like stunned goldfish.

"Evie! What on earth?" Hannah came dashing out of the back kitchen and did a double take at the sight of the shattered glass and purple slush now splattered across the floor. She looked at the customers. Then Evie. Then back at the customers again. "I am SO sorry, folks," she said, smiling nervously. "I guess we're still learning the ropes here. No harm done."

As everyone turned away and the hubbub of chat picked up again, Hannah grabbed the brush and shovel she kept handy and got down on her hands and knees to clean up the mess. "You know you're not supposed to be lifting trays," Hannah said. "Or making orders! And especially not today when we've got the Best Café Contest judge coming any moment." She sighed. "Why don't you go out and play in the yard?"

"By myself?" Evie felt her lip wobble. *Don't cry, Wonder Waitress!* she told herself. *Superhero serving staff never cry!* "But I LOVE helping out in the diner," she said.

Hannah looked up. "I know, but—"

"And I'm so sorry about the mess. But making drinks and desserts is so fun. Did I tell you about the amazing new ice cream sundae I've invented? It's got popping candy and—"

"Later, Evie," Hannah interrupted. "Tell me at dinner, okay? But in the meantime, if you really want to help, maybe you could go stack the strawberry saucepots in the storeroom cupboard. I need to put a new stock order in today and it'll be easier to count them if you pile them up."

Evie blinked at her stepmom. *Stacking sauce-pots in the back storeroom—ALONE?* Her shoulders drooped and she felt the tears welling up in her eyes again. *That's almost as bad as playing in the yard.* "Okay," Evie mumbled, heading for the door to the kitchen. "No problem."

Hannah was always doing this. Dreaming up desperately dull jobs for Evie to do to keep her safely out of the diner, like drying dishes in the kitchen, or polishing the cutlery, or counting the bags of little wooden spoons that they served with the ice cream. (For the record, they had 3,981 spoons last time Evie checked.) But checking stock in the store-room was the most boring work of all. *There's no one to talk to*, Evie thought as she walked down the cor-ridor. *And not even a window to see people passing by.*

But five minutes later, as Evie was stretching up on tiptoes to add another bottle to her super-tall tower of strawberry sauce bottles, she heard a shriek. *Huh?* She listened. *Uh-oh, that sounds like at least a six on the Scale of Super-Cranky Customer Meltdowns!*

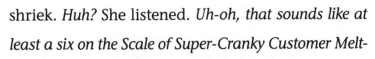

THE SCALE OF SUPER-CRANKY CUSTOMER MELTDOWNS

10. Spilling order all over customer— **Full Eruption!**

9. Fly in the soup

8. Dogs in the diner

7. Receiving the wrong check

6. Unavailable menu items

5. Receiving the wrong order

4. Order too cold

3. Order too hot

2. Don't like the music

1. Slow service—**Smoking Volcano**

She dropped the sauce bottle she was holding and was about to bound through the storeroom door to go sort it out when she paused. *Would Hannah want me to help after my purple slushie disaster?* She chewed on her lip for a moment or two and considered. *Probably not.* She sighed. But then there was another scream. Even louder than the first. *On the other hand, this definitely sounds like a job for Wonder Waitress!* And she dived for the door.

CHAPTER 2

Every customer in the diner had turned to look at the table in the middle of the room, where her stepmom Hannah was trying to calm a red-faced, screaming preschooler.

"I am so sorry," Hannah was shouting, trying to be heard over the little boy's cries. "I know it says we have gummy bears on the list of ice cream sundae toppings, but you see, we've run out." Hannah pushed her curly hair out of her eyes and smiled at the little boy's mom, who was doing her best to distract her son with a cuddly dog toy. "We've only been open a few weeks," Hannah explained. "And we've never run a diner before, so we're still learning about how to order the right things at the right time, and—"

But she was drowned out by the little boy howling even louder.

Okay, time for Wonder Waitress to take charge! "Hey—don't cry," Evie said, squeezing in front of her stepmom and smiling at the boy. "I can see you really like dogs," she added, pointing to his shirt. "Me too!"

The boy stopped hollering for a moment and blinked at her, his bright red face glistening with tears. Then he looked down at the picture of the dachshund on his shirt.

"That's such a cool dog," Evie said. "I used to know one just like that. It lived next door to us before we moved here. It was called Peanut because that's exactly what it looked like—a giant peanut on legs!"

The little boy giggled.

Evie's stepmom coughed. "Um—thanks, Evie. But I've got this—see, I was just explaining to the folks here that we don't have any gummy bears left today, but we do have . . . banana chips! Yummy!"

The little boy's smile vanished.

Not yummy at all! Evie thought. *I wouldn't swap gummy bears for banana chips either— Uh-oh, he's about to go into "full-on erupting volcano" mode again unless Wonder Waitress can put out the flames!* "Wait!" she said, stopping him in his tracks. "How about I fix you one of my favorite desserts. It's called a Pup Cone!"

The little boy cocked his head to one side. "What dat?"

"It's a doggie dessert," Evie said. "It's made with chocolate ice cream and chocolate drops and it looks exactly like a puppy. Hey—maybe you could come up to the counter and help me make it?"

Hannah gasped. "Now, Evie, I really don't think—"

"Oh, that would be wonderful," the little boy's mom interrupted. "Peter would love to make his own dessert. Perhaps we could get it to go," she added, gathering up her purse and coat, "while I pay the check."

Evie tried not to catch her stepmom's eye as she led Peter behind the counter.

Evie rarely got to make ice cream sundaes. Which she thought was totally unfair, because, as Evie reminded her stepmom every day: "Kids have THE best dessert ideas on the planet," and "Kids also eat the most desserts, so we know what tastes good." But Hannah never listened. It was as though her ears were full of marshmallows.

"Here, stand on this," Evie told Peter, as she slid a little step in front of him. "Because the counter is WAY too high. I think it must have been made for giraffes. Now, let's get you a big scoop of chocolate ice cream," she said, spooning out a giant ball from the ice cream trays in front of them. She slopped it onto a cone, then reached for the chocolate drop box. "Now, I'll show you how to arrange the drops to make your pup's ears and eyes and, oh yeah—we'll need a squirt of strawberry sauce for its mouth."

★ HOW TO MAKE A PUP CONE ★

- Scoop a big ball of chocolate ice cream onto a cone.

- Use mini marshmallows and chocolate buttons for the eyes and nose (stick onto your ice cream with chocolate sauce).

- Cover another chocolate drop or marshmallow with strawberry sauce, or use a red icing pen for the tongue.

- Use large chocolate buttons or edible wafer paper for the ears.

- Eat quick, before it melts!

As the little boy set to work, Evie looked around the room. *Uh-oh! There sure are a lot of impatient-looking customers today. That's bad, what with the Best Café Contest judge arriving at any moment . . .*

Evie's stepmom had been talking of nothing else all week. The annual Golden Coffee Cup Best Café Contest was a big deal in Lime Bay, the town they'd recently moved to. "And winning the contest would put us on the map," Hannah had explained. But the trouble was, they didn't know what the judge looked like or when they'd appear.

Evie glanced over at a family of four in the corner: a mom and a dad and two blond-haired daughters who looked around Evie's age. *I wonder if those kids will be in my class at school? Maybe I could go say hi?* She smiled at them, but they scowled back. Then the mom checked her watch and rolled her eyes. *Oops, I hope that lady isn't the Best Café Contest judge.* Evie peered at the woman some more. *Nah, probably only a regular customer getting a bit fed up waiting for her order.* Evie looked around for her stepmom, but she had disappeared back into the kitchen. Evie puffed out her cheeks. *If Hannah let me help more, then everyone would get served much quicker.*

When Evie's dad and stepmom had told her about their plan to move to the coastal town of Lime Bay and open a diner, it had all seemed like such a fairy tale. Sea, sand, and ice cream sundaes! But it turned out that owning a beach-front café did not mean you got to sit around eating desserts for half the day before heading off to play in the surf. Running a café was hard work, with demanding customers and lots of icky mess to clean up. And her parents got zero free time to hang out with her. *Which is why I want to help more,* Evie thought. *It's the only time I get to see them!*

"Hey, want me to show you how to turn a napkin into a dog, too?" she asked Peter, who had now finished creating his Pup Cone. She picked up a paper napkin from the pile on the counter and began folding. "See, these are its ears, and this is its nose."

She reached for a pen. "And we can draw some crazy googly eyes on it, like this."

HOW TO TURN A NAPKIN INTO A DOG

You will need:

- A square napkin (or trim a rectangular napkin into a square)

- A black felt tip pen

How to do it:

- Fold your square into a triangle shape.

- With the folded edge at the top, fold down the right-hand corner into an ear shape, then repeat on the left.

- Fold up the bottom points of the triangle on both sides.

- Then fold down the tip of the front triangle you just made to form the nose.

- Color the nose in.

- Draw eyes and decorate the ears.

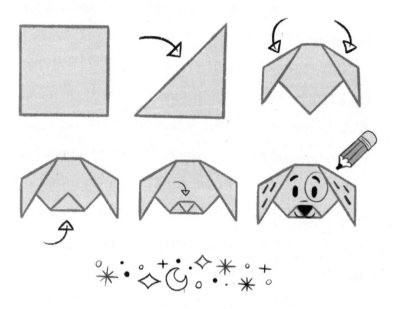

Peter giggled.

"Here, take it home with you," Evie said, as the boy grabbed his Pup Cone and jumped down from the stool to go join his mom who was waiting by the door. Evie waved to them both as they left the diner.

"Hi, could I have our check, please?"

Evie looked around and saw a red-haired girl, about her own age, standing at the counter. She remembered seeing her come in earlier. The girl smiled at her. And Evie noticed a large gap between her two front teeth. It made Evie want to smile back even more.

"Um—sure." Evie wasn't supposed to sort out the checks by herself . . . *But Hannah's in the kitchen and I REALLY want to show her how helpful I can be. Especially today with the Best Café Contest judges about to arrive.* "Er . . . table three, right?" Evie squinted at the board of checks. Trying to read her stepmom's writing was like deciphering ancient Egyptian hieroglyphs. "I think this is it—"

But the girl already had the right money ready. "And this is for you," the girl said, putting extra on the counter. "Bye." She turned and raced off outside to join an older lady in a long flowery frock and a fancy hat with purple flowers on the top. *Shame the girl was in a rush to go. She looked kind of fun.*

Evie reached down to pick up the money, and that's when she saw it. "Hey—wait!" she called after the girl. "You forgot your book." But the girl, who was outside now, didn't seem to hear her. Evie picked up the book and turned it over in her hands. The pages were made of thick cream-colored paper with golden edges. And on the front was a picture of three young women with long hair and fussy frocks. "Happily Ever After Stories," Evie read the title aloud, and the book seemed to wobble in her hands. *Huh? That's weird!*

"Excuse me!"

Evie looked up to find the mom from the table with the two blond girls, staring across the counter at her. "We're STILL waiting for our order!"

"Oh, sorry. I'm sure my stepmom's fetching it now. But you see, the last customer left this behind." Evie waggled the book in front of the woman. "And it looks really old and valuable, so will you please excuse me for one moment, while I go and try to return it?"

The woman gave a loud huff. "I'm sorry, but we don't want to wait. Please go fetch your mom and tell her we'd like our order now! Oh, and I see you've got cards here for customers to give feedback," she said, taking one out of the box on the counter and snatching up a mini pencil from the pot next to it. "Well, I definitely have some advice on how your diner could improve—though this card's probably not big enough for all I have to say!"

But Evie was already rushing around to the customer side of the counter, to try to catch up with the red-haired girl who owned the book.

Unfortunately, the floor tiles were still slightly sticky from the purple slushie disaster, and as Evie's foot made contact with them, she found herself sticking, then tripping, then slipping, then—"Watch it!" Evie tried to warn the woman, who was now leaning on the counter furiously filling in her feedback card, completely oblivious to the fact that Evie was heading straight for her.

Evie closed her eyes and waited for the—

CRASH!

CHAPTER 3

The woman went flying. The feedback cards followed. Then the mini pencil pot rolled neatly along the counter edge and plopped (perfectly) onto the woman's head.

Evie picked herself up off the floor, trying not to giggle. *Whoa! I couldn't have done that if I'd tried.* Then she remembered that "Wonder Waitress" was supposed to be HELPING customers, not attacking them. Especially today, when the diner was expecting the mystery judge in Lime Bay's Best Café Contest!

"I am so sorry," Evie said to the woman, who was still sitting on the ground as if she couldn't quite believe what had happened.

"Evie!" Hannah had appeared from the kitchen. She stood rooted to the spot, horror flashing across her face. "Not again! What on—how? I mean, why?

Oh, gosh, please let me help you up." She sprang forward to offer the woman a hand.

But the woman waved it away. "I'm fine!" she snapped, stumbling to her feet. Her husband and daughters had appeared by her side now, fussing and muttering. The two girls were glaring at Evie.

"This place is unsafe!" the woman said. "I can't believe you let a child work here."

"Oh, but Evie doesn't work here," Hannah said. "She just likes to help and—"

"She shouldn't be helping!" the woman interrupted. She pointed a long, bony finger at Hannah. "You're a bad mom and a terrible diner owner!"

Evie gasped. *That's not fair! Hannah's lovely.*

"Please, won't you let me make it up to you," Hannah said, stepping in between Evie and the family. "We won't charge you for lunch. And perhaps you could come back tomorrow and have another meal, on the house."

Noooo! Evie wanted to yell. *They're mean!*

The woman snorted. "I will NEVER set foot in

here again! And I shall tell ALL my friends how awful this place is. Come on, Edward! Girls!" she added, nodding to her husband and daughters to follow her.

"Well, that went well," Hannah said after they had gone. Then she turned to Evie.

Uh-oh! Evie closed her eyes and waited for it. The full-on-face-in-a-wind-tunnel-force-ten-megablaster telling-off! Hannah was like a dormant volcano. She didn't blow often, but when she did . . .

Strangely, it didn't happen.

Evie opened one eye and saw her stepmom crouched down, picking up the feedback cards and putting the mini pencils back in their pot. Evie's heart sank at the look on Hannah's face. *This is even worse than a telling-off.* This is what her older cousin Dylan called "silent disappointment." The killer weapon in all parents' armories.

"Are you going to tell Dad?" Evie asked.

"Tell me what?" Her dad appeared in the doorway, his arms full of groceries and his hair and clothes smelling of sea air. "Tell me that we've got the BEST life ever and you're both so glad we moved to Lime Bay?"

Hannah sighed. "Not exactly."

Dad looked at Evie. "More mishaps?"

"Just a couple." Evie picked up the old book from where she'd dropped it when she'd crashed into the customer. Something about her dad's cheerful face made her suddenly feel a little angry. It was okay for him. He was a chef. He was allowed to help out in the diner. He got to play with flour and sugar and sprinkles all day. And moving to a new town was easy for him too, because he had brought his best friend with him—Hannah!—and they got to hang out together all the time. And even though Evie liked the diner, she missed her old life—her friends, her school, and Peanut the dog who had lived next door to their old house.

And most of all, she missed spending time with her parents!

"I want to help out more," Evie said, and the

book in her hand gave a little jiggle. Evie glanced at it, but she was too mad at everything to pay it much attention. "I know I drop stuff," she said. "But I'm also really good at making desserts. Like last night—I made this awesome new ice cream sundae called Toffee-Topper-Space-Hopper. And it's got blue moon ice cream and popping candy and mini meringues and toffee sauce and it would definitely win the Best Café Contest if you served it to the judge . . . But you won't even give me a chance to show you!" Her voice was getting louder now, and the book seemed to shake even more at the sound of it. But she was WAY too upset to look at it.

Evie straightened her back, gritted her teeth, and stuck her chin out. The book was juddering wildly. Not that Evie's parents noticed. They were too busy smiling nervously at the customers whose eyes were glued to the scene unfolding in front of them. *I don't care if people see!* Evie thought. Frustration and loneliness were fizzing up inside her like a giant kid-size bottle of shaken soda pop. And then suddenly it burst out of the top. "If you won't let me help in the diner," Evie said, her voice shaking as much as the book, "THEN I WISH I COULD GO BACK HOME!" At the sound of the word *wish*, there was a loud crack and a flash of silver, then—

"You tell 'em, kiddo!" shouted a sweet female voice from behind her. "Nobody makes Evie unhappy and gets away with it! But don't worry; we've got your back. These two rotten rascals aren't going to win!"

CHAPTER 4

Evie spun around to find a young woman in a sparkly pink dress, with her hands on her hips and a determined look on her face. "Isn't that right, Agent R and Agent B?" she added. And from behind her, two more young women stepped forward.

"Right on, Agent C!" said the one with impossibly long silver hair, which she tossed over her shoulder with a glare at Evie's parents.

"And not even a pet to comfort her," said the

third young woman, who was peering around the room from behind thick brown bangs. "Everyone knows that a home isn't a home without a beast of your own!"

Huh? Evie stared at them, her mouth open, her eyes wide.

"Okay, time out!" Evie's dad dumped the groceries he was carrying onto the counter and put his arm around Evie's shoulders. "Show's over, folks," he added to the customers who were still watching. "Sorry about the fuss, please go back to your meals." Strangely he didn't even glance at the three young women, who were now glaring at him so hard Evie expected them to leave scorch marks on his face.

"Moving to a new town is never easy," her dad said. "I know you miss your friends. But you'll soon make new ones—oh, sorry, honey—one moment—" He looked across the tables to where a customer was trying to get his attention. "I think that gentleman needs something. I'll just go see to him . . ."

"Your dad's right," Hannah said. "Everything will be better soon." She gave Evie a quick hug. "We'll talk about this again tonight. I promise."

"We certainly will!" said the young woman with the long silver hair, who was waggling her finger at Hannah now. "Don't think you've heard the last of this, missy!"

Missy? Evie's eyes opened wide. No customer had ever called Hannah that before. She waited for her stepmom to respond. But she didn't even look up from the table she'd started to clear. Hannah then picked up the dirty dishes and walked off toward the kitchen. Evie frowned. *It's as though she can't see them.* And with their fussy frocks and big hair, it would be impossible to miss them . . . *They look like they've escaped from a Princess Barbie dress-up party!*

Evie smiled. After blowing her top she felt a bit better now, and she LOVED greeting customers— she practiced in front of the mirror sometimes. *And it doesn't look like my parents are going to welcome this group anytime soon, which is super strange, especially on Best Café Contest day—they could be the judges!*

Evie straightened her shirt and smoothed down her shorts. "Hi, welcome to Brown's Diner," she said to the three young women. "Did you want to eat? I can find you a table."

"Oh, bless her cotton socks," the one with the thick brown bangs whispered. "She's so kind."

"Too kind!" said the one with long silver hair.

"Though hard work never hurt anyone," said the first young woman in the pink dress. "So long as it's rewarded fairly."

"Er . . . I guess," Evie said. "Would you like to see some menus?"

"Menus? Oh, we haven't time to eat," the one in the pink dress said. "We've got work to do. Wait— didn't we introduce ourselves?"

The other two looked at each other. "I think we forgot," said the quieter one with the thick brown bangs.

"Not again!" The young woman with the long silver hair rolled her eyes and snorted. "Okay, listen up, kiddo. Here's the deal. We're H.E.A.R.T.!"

"That's the Happily Ever After Rescue Team," added the one in the pink frock. "I'm Agent C, that's C for Cinderella!"

Evie tried not to laugh. "What, like in the storybook?"

But Agent C didn't hear. She'd pulled out two pink scarves from the pockets of her dress and was using them to do some strange cheerleader pom-pom routine.

"I'm Rapunzel," the silver-haired one said, flicking her locks so wildly she blew a few napkins off a nearby table. "Also known as Agent R."

"And I'm Agent B, but folks call me Beauty," the quieter girl said, peeping out from behind her bangs. "I may be gentle, but I can be a real beast!" She made a pouncing lion face and held her hands up like claws.

Evie took a step back. *Okay, this is getting super weird. Maybe I should call Dad . . .*

"We're here to make sure you get your *happily ever after!*" Agent C said. "And from what we just heard, that means we need to get you out of the clutches of your wicked stepmother!"

"Oh, she's not wicked," Evie said. "She's really kind."

But Agent C wasn't listening. "Now, where do you keep your pumpkins?" She darted behind the counter and began opening cupboards and looking in drawers. "Nope. Nothing. I'll try the kitchen . . . Through here, is it?"

Evie gasped. "No! Stop!—Hannah's in the kitchen!" *And she does not like customers going back there.* Evie was about to go block the way when she felt a sudden hard tug on her hair. "Yow!"

"Not sure what we'll do with this," Agent R said, giving Evie's hair another pull. "WAY too short. If they lock you in a tower, you'll never escape with that!"

"Escape?" Evie frowned. "Oh, wait—did you hear all that stuff I said about wanting to go home? I didn't mean I was going to run away. I just wanted my parents to let me help out in the diner more and—"

"Maybe I could glue some of my own hair onto yours," Agent R said, not listening. She picked up the ends of her own silver tresses and held them next to Evie's. "Nah, your hair color's ALL wrong. And your wicked stepmom will notice. But I'll fetch some dye and we'll make it work."

"I don't want to dye it!" Evie said. *Well, I'd really like purple hair, but NO WAY would Hannah let me do that.*

But Agent R had already jogged off outside, her long silver hair fanning out like a swirly cape behind her.

"Hair dye? Tish and fish!" Agent B tutted. "It's always about hair with her. When of course what you really need to solve any problem is just a big fluffy dog. Anything is *paw-sible* when you have a pet of your own." She tucked her dark locks behind her ears, and Evie noticed she was wearing sparkly diamond studs shaped like little paw prints. "Your parents will treat you so much better with a beast by your side. I'll go find one."

"Um, that's kind of you," Evie said. "But Hannah doesn't like dogs. And anyway, they're not allowed in the diner—especially not today. See, we've entered the Best Café Contest and a judge could come any moment and everything has to be perfect and—"

But Agent B had already trotted out the door, her green dress flapping in the breeze.

For a moment Evie stood there, her mouth open and her eyes wide. *What just happened here? Did I get a bump on the head when I crashed into that customer?* Evie remembered a boy at school who had banged his head in gym and started talking about llamas in pajamas and tap-dancing raccoons. *Or maybe I'm just asleep and this is all a crazy dream?*

She pinched herself to check. *Ow!* Nope. Pinching did NOT help.

"Two blueberry muffins and a large cappuccino," Evie's dad said, scribbling on an order pad as he made his way back through the tables. "And such a nice gentleman. He was telling me all about how Lime Bay got its name. It's such an interesting story and—hey, Evie, are you okay? You look pale. And what's that you're holding so tightly?" He peered at the cover of the book Evie still held in her hands. "It looks old . . . fairy tales, is it?"

Evie had forgotten about the book. She glanced down at the picture on the front cover of the three young women with big hair and fussy frocks. She blinked. Then looked again. *No, surely it couldn't be?* "It's them!" she muttered, staring at the picture some more. "Except, it can't be. Can it?" She looked at her dad. "Is this a dream?"

But her dad's reply was drowned out by a loud shout from the kitchen. "Found one!" And Agent C came racing back, holding a large potato above her head like a soccer ball. "I know it's not actually a pumpkin," Agent C said. "But if I can just remember my fairy godmother's spell, this is going to make THE perfect escape coach. Now all we need are some mice."

CHAPTER 5

"Mice?" Evie's eyes goggled. *Mice would NEVER be allowed in the diner. Especially not today! Hannah would freak!*

"What did you say, honey?" Her dad was looking at her now. "Something about mice?"

But Evie was distracted by Agent C, who had begun a strange dance, wiggling and jiggling around the potato, which she had laid on the diner floor. Not that Evie's dad seemed to have noticed.

"There are definitely no mice in the diner," he said, dropping his voice a little, so the customers couldn't hear. Then he looked where Evie was looking—directly at Agent C—but he still didn't seem to see the strange young woman. "Nope, I don't see any, thank goodness! Now, I'd better go fix that gentleman's order." He popped his pencil behind his ear and his pad back in his pocket and smiled at Evie. "Why don't you go play in the yard, honey. Don't forget you've got that brand-new trampoline out there," he added, as he headed off to the kitchen.

Evie didn't reply; she couldn't drag her eyes away from Agent C, who was now waggling her arms around her head as though she were being attacked by a swarm of wasps. Evie swallowed a giggle.

"Would you mind not staring," Agent C puffed. "My magic spells go wonky when people watch!"

But that was the weird thing. No one *was* watching. Evie glanced around the room. Not one customer's head was turned toward Agent C. It was as though it was perfectly normal for a young woman in a shiny pink frock to be dancing around a potato in the middle of a diner.

"Hey, look! I got some!" Agent R came jogging back into the diner, waving a small cardboard box in the air with the words DARE TO DYE on its label. "Now, let's get you comfy," she said, pulling Evie across to a stool by the counter. "The instructions say the dye works in thirty minutes." She ripped open the box and held a little brown bottle up to the light. "Imagine, in half an hour you'll have lovely silver hair, just like me!"

What? Noooo! Evie wriggled off the seat. "I don't want to dye my hair. And even if I did, there's no way Hannah would let me." She stopped speaking as the customers at a nearby table turned to look at her. *Huh?* She blinked back at them. Not one of them was looking at the agents. *You guys really can't see them, can you? You just think I'm talking to myself!* She glanced at the kitchen door; it was definitely time to fetch a grown-up, because this was all getting WAY too weird!

But just then, there was a loud bark and the scrabble of paws on the diner tiles. Evie turned to see a small brown dog come bounding through the door.

"Evie! Look! I found one!" Agent B said, following closely behind. "And, he's *paw-sitively* perfect!" Agent B threw her arms around the pup and pulled him close. "He was lost and alone and snuffling around the trash cans. He told me he's homeless without anyone to love him—I can speak dog don't you know," she added with a wink. "And I told him that I knew someone who would love him *fur-ever!* Come, give him a hug."

Evie froze. She LOVED dogs; they were her favorite sort of animal. Back home she used to walk her neighbor's dog Peanut every day. But a dog in the diner? *Hannah will flip!* Evie wasn't sure what to do. The right thing would be to go fetch her parents. *But the pup looks so soft and cuddly, and he has such* shiny eyes, and such a waggly tail and, and—maybe just one quick hug before he has to leave. "Oh wow, you're so friendly." Evie giggled as the puppy jumped into her arms and licked her cheek.

"Aw, you're made for each other," Agent B cooed. "What will you name him?"

"Fudge," Evie murmured without thinking. That was the name she'd picked out years ago when she'd first daydreamed about having a dog of her own. For a few moments she stayed that way, eyes closed, breathing in the wriggly little pup's warm, doggy smell, thinking about how lovely it would be if Fudge really did belong to her. *We could go for walks on the beach and swim in the sea. And I could make you a little jacket for the winter to keep you cozy. And you could sleep at the bottom of my bed and—* But then she remembered where she was. She opened her eyes. Her shoulders drooped and she sighed. "He's lovely, but dogs aren't actually allowed in the diner."

Beauty's reply was drowned out by a strange PHWAT noise, and a tiny puff of green smoke wisped past Evie's nose.

"Oh bother!" Agent C snapped. "Not again." The potato at her feet had vanished and in its place was a strange and rather green-looking—

"Plate of french fries?" Evie whispered.

"Yes, yes, magic is not as easy as it looks," Agent C said. "Especially not when everyone is watching." She folded her arms and puffed out her cheeks. "I'll have to find another potato now. And then there's still the problem of the mice. I need them to turn into horses to pull your escape coach—or do I?" She stopped talking as her eyes spotted the dog. She cocked her head to one side. "You know HE would make a perfectly good horse."

"Paws off!" Beauty jumped in front of Evie and the pup, with her hands on her hips. "I'm a whisker away from getting cranky now. Fudge is Evie's protector beast. He's her BFFF—that's Best Furry Friend *Fur-ever*," she added, with a smile at Evie. "And anyway, Agent C, your magic skills are so bad you're likely to change him into a hamster instead of a horse."

Agent C's face turned red. "That's not true!"

"Well, it wouldn't be the first time," Agent B said. "Remember that poor cat. You turned it into a balloon!"

"I turned it straight back again," Agent C said.

"Not before that mean kid with the pin nearly popped it!" Agent B shook her head. "It was almost a *cat-astrophe*! If I hadn't rescued it, goodness knows what might have happened."

"Well, I think you're both ridiculous," Agent R said, tossing her long silvery locks over her shoulder. "Everyone knows the only things you need to escape from any bad situation are a strong pair of arms"—she flexed her muscles to show Evie just how strong hers were—"and a good head of hair. Now come on, Evie, it's time for your makeover."

She waggled the bottle of dye. "Oh, and I've just had the best idea! We'll dye the pup's fur to match yours. It would definitely improve his look."

Evie gasped. "You don't dye dogs!" She backed away, holding Fudge closer.

"Absolutely not!" Agent B glared at Rapunzel. "If anyone needs a makeover, it's you! That hair of yours is *paw-ful*! It's always tripping me up."

"Well, maybe if you trimmed your bangs," Agent R snapped back, "you could see where you're going. Really, Beauty, they look like a crazy set of drapes!"

Agent C sniggered, and suddenly all three agents were bickering and yelling at one another and not listening to Evie one little bit.

"Oh boy!" Evie whispered to Fudge, hugging him closer. "What a noise! How can I make them stop arguing?"

As if in answer, the little pup twisted his head toward the door, and Evie saw a girl slipping into the diner with a large denim bag slung across her shoulders and a big old floppy hat pulled down low over her face. She peeped out from under the brim, her eyes hidden behind giant dark sunglasses. "Don't worry," she whispered to Evie. "I got this!" And she gave her a wide grin.

Huh? Evie frowned. There was something familiar about the girl's gap-toothed smile.

CHAPTER 6

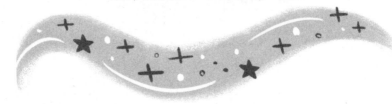

The girl in the hat climbed onto a chair. "Listen up, everyone!" she shouted. "We've got a major crisis outside!"

Conversation stopped. The room froze. And every head in the diner turned to look at her, including the Agents of H.E.A.R.T.

The girl swallowed a few times, as though she wasn't sure what to say next. Then she coughed and cleared her throat. "So, er . . . first up, we've got a hairdressing sort of an emergency," she said. "There's a teenager outside who is on her way to a party and her French braid has come undone. Can anyone here fix it?"

A few of the diners exchanged confused looks with one another. But Agent R's hand shot straight up.

"I do French braids! Where is she?"

"She's down the street," the girl in the hat replied. "Just go out the door, turn left, then keep on going until you find her."

Oh wow! She can see them, too, Evie thought. *I'm not going crazy after all.*

Agent R didn't need asking twice. As she jogged off, tossing her long, silvery hair behind her, the mysterious girl pulled out a cell phone and tapped a couple of its buttons . . . DONG! DONG! DONG! A loud chime began to sound. Evie watched as Agent C gasped and clasped her hands to her chest, counting as every chime rang out. At the twelfth dong, she let out a tiny squeal. "Midnight? Oh no! I must leave at once!" She rushed for the door, stumbling slightly and leaving a small glass shoe behind her.

Whoa! That's so clever, Evie thought. *She's using their stories to give them a time-out!*

The girl in the hat looked like she was about to get down from her chair when she suddenly spotted Beauty. "Um—I don't remember you from last time." She glanced at Evie. "Who is she?" she whispered. "Because I don't know how to get rid of her."

But Evie knew exactly what was required. "Um, the diner cat has vanished!" Evie blurted out. "Is anyone free to go look for it?"

"Ah!" the girl in the hat murmured. "I guess she's Beauty, then."

A couple of the customers started to get to their feet. But Beauty was already at the door. "Stand back!" she yelled to the room of people who couldn't see her. "I'll find the cat! What does it look like, Evie?"

"It's a tabby," the girl in the hat said, before Evie could reply. "And it answers to the name of Fancy Pants!"

Evie tried not to laugh.

"What a lovely name," Beauty cooed. "And do not worry, Evie. I shall find your little Fancy Pants for you." And she swept out the door.

"A diner cat?" Evie heard one of the customers say. "Are animals even allowed in a café?" A few people were staring at Fudge now.

"Thanks, everyone!" the girl in the hat said. "This was just . . . um . . . a drill. You know, like, er . . ."

"Fire drill at school?" Evie suggested, pulling Fudge closer. "But for pets—and—hairstyling problems."

"Exactly!" the girl said. "But it's good to know that if there is a hair crisis, or a cat goes missing, there are good folks like you who will be able to help."

The diners didn't look convinced. And Evie could hear a few mutterings of "Kids!" and "What a crazy place this is!" as they went back to their meals.

The girl climbed off her chair and stood awkwardly in front of Evie with her head down.

"That was so awesome," Evie whispered. "I didn't think anyone else could even see them. How did you know what to do?"

The girl sighed, then reached up and pulled off her hat and glasses and stuffed them into her bag.

"It's you!" Evie said. "The girl who left her book on the counter. Look, I have it here . . ." Evie held the book of fairy tales out. But the red-haired girl didn't take it. "I tried to catch up with you to return it," Evie said. "But then I had an accident with one of the customers."

"Thanks for trying . . . I guess." But the girl still didn't take the book. She looked at her feet. "My name is Iris Flowers," she mumbled. "And I kind of owe you an apology."

"You do?" Evie frowned. "Why?"

"I'll tell you. But first we've got to get out of here." Iris peeped through the window out onto the street. "The Agents of H.E.A.R.T. will be back any moment. They never stay away long."

"Evie?"

Hannah had reappeared with a tray of coffee cups. "Oh my goodness!" she gasped, gazing at the puppy in Evie's arms. "A dog in the diner? Where on earth did that come from?"

"Er . . . the street?" Evie snuggled Fudge closer. "But look, he's so cute. See, he's wagging his tail."

"B-b-but dogs are not allowed in here!" Hannah said, glancing around the room to see if anyone had noticed. "What if the Best Café Contest judge spots it? Please, will you take it outside onto the terrace; its owners are probably looking for it."

"No, it's homeless," Evie said. *I know, because*

Beauty told me and she speaks dog! she wanted to add.

"Well, if it is, it might have fleas!" Hannah grimaced. "Go on, now, take it outside."

"I'll come with you," Iris said.

Hannah smiled at her. "Thank you. Are you here with your family?"

"I *was* here with my granny, earlier," Iris said. "She has the flower stall across the street." Iris pointed through the window. "See, over there, by the boardwalk . . . She's the lady in the large hat."

"Oh yes, I see her." Hannah nodded. "It's a very nice hat."

Evie looked, too. It was the older lady she'd seen before, wearing the sun hat with purple flowers on the top. She was wrapping a bunch of roses for a customer.

"Well, I hope you girls can find the dog's owner," Hannah said, holding the door open for them. "Someone must be very worried about it."

No, they're not! Evie frowned at her stepmom.

Because Fudge is a stray! But Hannah had already turned back to the counter.

Evie followed Iris out onto the café's terrace, with Fudge still in her arms. "Here's your book, by the way."

"Oh yeah, thanks." Iris took it, then held it out in front of her between one finger and thumb, as though it might bite her. She looked like she was about to say something more, when suddenly she pointed up the street. "Uh-oh! There's Agent C!" She pushed the book into her bag and grabbed Evie's arm. "Come on! We've got to run. Quick, before she spots us."

CHAPTER 7

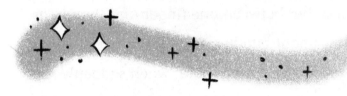

"This way!" Iris shouted as she darted across the street. "We'll lose her on the beach; there are loads of people down there."

"Wait up! I should tell Hannah where I'm going . . . And what about Fudge?" Evie followed behind, trying to keep hold of the wriggling pup, while Iris raced ahead. As Evie reached the beach, her feet sank into the warm sand and her heart stopped pounding. She wiggled her toes in her sandals and snuggled her face against Fudge's soft coat, and for a moment she forgot all about the craziness of the Agents of H.E.A.R.T.

"Hurry!" Iris came running back to find her. "We've got to keep moving."

"But it's so calm here," Evie said, her feet sinking deeper into the sand with every step. "And why do we need to run away? I mean, I know the agents are a little cranky with each other. But they seem fun. Can't we slow down just for a second—and hey, you said you owed me an apology, but you never explained why."

"Oh yeah, that." Iris looked around for a moment, scanning the beach up and down, left and right, then nodded. "Okay, I think Agent C must have gone the other way. I'll explain everything, but we've got to keep walking. Trust me, the Agents of H.E.A.R.T. can appear from nowhere."

And why does that matter? Evie frowned at her. "I don't understand why you hate them so much—I mean, they're actual real, live magical creatures!"

Evie's eyes sparkled. "Like unicorns and pixies and mermaids and—"

"Yeah, right!" Iris rolled her eyes.

"But they are! Agent B even gave me Fudge," Evie went on. "I've always wanted a dog, so she can't be that bad. And anyway . . . what about this apology you owe me?"

Iris was quiet for a moment. She poked at a blob of seaweed lying in the sand with her sneaker toe, then sighed. "Your name's Evie, right? I think I heard your mom call you that."

Evie nodded.

"Okay, Evie, well you see, the Agents of H.E.A.R.T. have been bothering me, too—ever since my granny brought this home." She opened her bag and pulled out the fairy tale book. "I thought it was just a regular book, until one afternoon when Gammy—that's what I call my granny—was asking me to do some chores and I said I wished I could go play ball instead. Next thing I knew, Agent R and Agent C arrived—Beauty didn't come visit me, which is odd, but anyway, they told me that of course 'I should go to the ball!' Only they got the wrong sort of ball." Iris shook her head. "They thought I wanted to go to some fairy-tale party. Next thing I knew, I was in this weird 'coach and horses' thing, wearing a big puffy dress and way too much hairspray, galloping along the street to the ball."

Evie tried not to laugh. She didn't want to offend Iris, but it did sound kind of funny.

"But of course, there was no ball," Iris said. "Just the ballpark, where I had to get out in front of all the other kids looking like I'd just been to a costume party. It was SO embarrassing!" Iris pushed her red hair out of her eyes. "And when I got home the agents were still there. And it's not like they're fun to have around. They're always squabbling. I thought me and my cousin Zak argued a lot, but the Agents of H.E.A.R.T. can't agree on anything."

"Why can't other people see them?" Evie asked.

"Kids can see them. They're just invisible to grown-ups. But I didn't know that at first. So when I tried telling Gammy about them she thought I was sick. She made me go lie down with a cold pack on my head—oh, wait!" She looked over Evie's shoulder. "I thought I just spotted Agent C again—that pink dress is hard to miss." She squinted to see better, then relaxed a little. "False alarm. It's just some woman shaking out a beach towel. Come on, let's get closer to the water. There are more kids there, so it'll be harder for her to spot us."

"But I still don't get why that matters," Evie said, as they dodged a group of preschoolers digging in the sand. "My arms are about to drop off, and I really need to get back to the diner."

"You can't!" Iris said. "The agents will find you."

"But I have to!" Evie was starting to feel a little grouchy now. "Today is a really important day. It's the Best Café Contest! The mystery judge could come at any moment and I REALLY want to help my stepmom win, because then she'll realize how awesome I am as a waitress and—" Just at that moment, Fudge turned and licked Evie's nose, and her grumpiness instantly turned into a giggle. "Ha! Maybe she'll be SO happy, she'll even let me keep Fudge!"

Iris grunted. "That sounds like a longshot. Your stepmom didn't look very keen on the pup." She reached over and stroked his head. "Which is weird, because he is cute."

"Exactly! So that's another reason why I need to get back, so Hannah can see how special Fudge is. And anyway, you made the agents vanish with your tricks, right?"

"Yeah, but those stunts never last long, which reminds me . . ." Iris pulled out the cell from her bag. "I have to get this back to Gammy."

"You still haven't told me why you owe me an apology."

"Oh yeah—that." Iris's face turned red. "You see, it's my fault that they're bothering you."

"Why?"

Iris scuffed the sand with her shoe and looked away. "Because I deliberately left the book in your diner," she said in a small voice. "I wanted to dump the agents onto some other kid. And I guess I chose you."

"What? No way!" Evie gazed at Iris, a strange squishy feeling in her tummy. "But that's so sneaky."

"I know." Iris's shoulders drooped and she looked at her feet. "I'm so, so sorry. I felt bad right away. That's why I came back. But by then I could see it was too late; the agents were already there. So, I went and fetched my disguise—the hat, the glasses . . . I knew they'd never fall for my tricks again if they recognized me." She looked at Evie with a glum expression. "Do you hate me?"

Evie stared at Iris for a long moment, her face stern. *Should I hate you? You could have asked for help instead of just dumping your problems on me. But then again, maybe it wasn't such a bad thing . . . I mean the agents did give me Fudge. And that trick that Agent C did when she turned the potato into french fries was kind of cool. And the diner was WAY more exciting when they appeared . . .* A slow smile spread over

Evie's face. "Nah, I don't hate you. The agents are fun."

Iris raised an eyebrow. "That's because you've only just met them. Trust me, they're even more irritating than my cousin Zak, and he's one of the most annoying people in Lime Bay."

"Just one question," Evie said. "Why did you choose me?"

"Well, I didn't, not really. You just happened to be in the wrong place at the right time." Iris sighed. "See, I was sitting with Gammy in the diner and getting all hot and bothered about the agents messing up another day, and then I just thought, 'I'm going to leave the book here for some other kid to deal with.' I was kind of hoping that the Pemberton twins might pick it up."

"Who?"

"Clara and Katie-Belle," Iris said. "Actually, they might even be more annoying than my cousin Zak. Didn't you see them? They were in the diner at the same time as me and my granny."

Before Evie could answer, they heard a shout—
"EVIE! There you are!"

"Huh?" She spun around to find Agent C limping over to them, her remaining glass slipper sinking into the sand and a large potato under her arm.

Iris groaned. "See! You turn your back for two minutes and they reappear."

"I've got some fabulous news!" Agent C said. "Oh—hello, you," she added, spotting Iris. "Nice to see you again. Now, look, Evie, I've found another potato. And wait until you see what else . . ." She pulled a short shimmery stick from up her sleeve and wafted it above her head, sending a little cloud of rainbows into the sky.

"That's her fairy godmother's wand," Iris whispered. "This is NOT going to end well!"

CHAPTER 8

Agent C began to spin, twirling around and around, sending more little rainbows into the air. "Magic, magic everywhere!" she sang. "Wicked stepmoms must beware!" Then suddenly she stopped spinning and staggered a little as she regained her balance. "Now, Evie, it's time to make your escape coach!"

"Yeah, about that . . . ," Evie began. "See, I don't actually want to escape. When I made that wish, what I was really asking for was to be able to help more in the diner and—"

But Agent C had already waved the wand over the potato.

PFFFF!

"Voilà! Your escape coach!" Agent C beamed.

"That's not a coach," Iris muttered. "That's a go-cart."

It was a go-cart. A tiny brown go-cart, with silver stripes down the side and sleigh bells at the front that tinkled softly in the breeze.

It looks like a baked potato on wheels, Evie thought. She was pretty sure there was no way she'd fit inside. And she was rather glad about that.

Agent C scratched her head with her wand, leaving rainbows in her hair. "Mmm, not quite what I was hoping for; pumpkins work so much better, but never mind. Now, let me see, what else do I need . . . Oh, yes—him!" And she plucked the puppy out of Evie's arms.

"No! Stop!" Evie tried to take him back, but

Agent C had already waved her wand, and—

PFFFF! The pup had vanished and in his place was—

"A donkey?" Evie gasped.

"Watch it!" Iris called. And the girls jumped out of the way as Fudge kicked out his back legs.

"Oh, how perfect!" Agent C cried, clapping her hands. "So much energy. He'll take you all the way home. Now, one more tap of the wand and he'll be attached to your coach!"

PFFF!

Evie stared in horror at the long purple ribbons that now tethered the pup to the go-cart. "Poor Fudge," she muttered, as he tossed his head to try to shake the ribbons off. "I bet he hates not being a dog anymore." A little tornado of irritability had started growing in her belly. Unkindness to animals was something Evie couldn't bear. She glared at Agent C. "You didn't even ask his permission. It's so unfair!"

Agent C blinked at Evie, as though she couldn't quite understand what Evie was complaining about. "But you can't escape from your wicked stepmother without a coach and horses."

"I don't want to escape!" Evie snapped. "I told you. My wish was about wanting to help more in the diner. But right now, more than anything, I WANT MY DOG BACK!"

Agent C looked at Fudge, who was now stamping his feet impatiently. "Mmm, yes, he's not the best-looking horse to pull your coach, is he? But I can't swap him for anything better, because I haven't got any mice, and besides, I haven't learned how to reverse a spell yet."

"What?" Evie's eyes opened wide. "You shouldn't be doing magic if you can't make it work!"

Iris coughed. "Now you're seeing why I wanted to run away."

Agent C pouted. "But doesn't practice make perfect?"

"I guess that's true." *Maybe magic is a bit like waitressing, because that's really hard to learn, too—carrying plates without dropping them, getting orders right, making sure you've added up the check correctly . . .*

Agent C's shoulders drooped, and she scuffed the sand with her single remaining glass slipper. "Magic is so much better than doing chores. Before I met my fairy godmother, you should have seen my hands: so red and sore! And my feet! They ached all the time. But not anymore . . ." She lifted her bare foot and waggled her toes at Evie. "See? No blisters! Perhaps I could teach you some magic, Evie. It might come in handy when your wicked stepmom is making you work—"

"Hannah's not wicked!" Evie interrupted. "And I WANT to help out more. I like helping." *But I guess if she WAS mean, it would be kind of you to want to save me from her.* "Maybe learning magic would be fun—but first you've got to fix my dog."

But Agent C's reply was drowned out by Fudge,

who suddenly let out a strange braying-barking sort of a noise. Then he stamped his feet and trotted away, pulling the cart with him.

"Wait!" Agent C cried. "You can't go yet. Evie's not on board!"

"Fudge!—Stop!" Evie dived after him, somehow managing to throw herself into the tiny go-cart as it trundled away.

"Oh, bravo!" Agent C called, clapping her hands and dancing on the spot. "You're going home after all. Enjoy your Happily Ever After, Evie. Goodbye! Goodbye, now!"

"What? No! I'm not going home," Evie tried to shout back. But her words were lost on the breeze.

The cart was moving faster now. It had reached the firmer sand closer to the sea, and Fudge was trotting much more quickly. Then he broke into a gallop and took off, zooming across the beach. "Ahhhh! Slow down, Fudge!" *Where are the brakes on this thing?*

The cart weaved this way and that, left and right, in and out of sunbathers and families and people doing sports. Heads turned. Fingers pointed. And parents grabbed small children out of the way. And all the time the little bells on the cart jingled, and Evie clung to the sides to prevent herself from falling out. "STOP, Fudge!" she yelled, gripping on tighter as the cart wobbled wildly. But nothing would stop Fudge. Nothing, that is—

—apart from the sudden whiff of hot dog!

The cart abruptly swerved left as Fudge followed his nose, heading straight for a hot dog stand. "Watch it!" Evie yelled as they hurtled toward two girls who were playing in the sand. "Get out of the way!" she shouted to them. But the girls just sat there, openmouthed and frozen in horror at the crazy vehicle looming in front of them.

CHAPTER 9

At the last minute, the girls dived to the side and there was a sudden, soft THWUP sound as Evie and the cart smashed into a mound of sand.

Wow! That's weird; the beach has turned itself upside down. Evie flicked the sand out of her eyes and wondered how the sea was managing to hang from the sky. *Oops, I think it's me that's the wrong way around.* She pulled herself up into a sitting position and shook a lump of wet sand out of her hair. And then she saw them: two extremely cranky and strangely similar faces, looming over her.

"You wrecked our sandcastles," one of the faces said.

"We were making a palace," the other added.

Evie shut her eyes. *I must have bumped my head, because I'm seeing double.*

"Evie! Are you okay?"

She heard Iris's voice and opened her eyes again.

"I tried to catch up with you," Iris puffed. "But you were going so fast."

Evie smiled at her. "Phew! There's only one of you. I thought for a moment my eyes had gone funny, because I was seeing two of everything."

"Ha!" snapped one of the angry faces, appearing around the side of Iris.

"We're twins, silly!" said the other.

Huh? Evie looked closer at the two girls. "Twins? That is so cool."

"I'll tell you what's NOT cool," said one of the twins, folding her arms and glaring at Evie, "is you and your stupid cart smashing our sandcastles!"

TIPS FOR BUILDING A MAGNIFICENT SAND PALACE BY CLARA AND KATIE-BELLE PEMBERTON

The Pemberton twins always ace any sandcastle contest! And here's how they do it.

You will need:

- Sand, water, and different size containers— buckets, beakers, pots, etc.

- Tools for carving and smoothing, such as kitchen utensils: spatulas, cake slicers, measuring spoons, pastry brushes (or paintbrushes), and straws. Or use Play-Doh tools.

- Spray bottle filled with water, to keep your sandcastle moist!

- For decoration materials, use natural decorations that you find on the beach so that you don't pollute the sand with man-made items left behind. Look for seaweed, feathers, driftwood, shells, sea glass, and pebbles.

Method:

- Choose a good location. Close to the sea so you can fetch water, but not too close or it'll be swept away.

- Get the sand/water balance correct. Experiment with different amounts of dampness in sand to see which hold together best.

- Try digging a hole to find damper sand.

- If you want a tall sculpture, pile up the sand until you have the height you want, then work down, shaping turrets, windows, doors, etc.

- Keep wetting your sand so it doesn't dry out and collapse.

- Decorate your sand palace with natural materials you've found on the beach.

- Make sure you take all your tools home with you.

"The cart?" Evie gasped. "Fudge! Is he okay?" She glanced around. "Um, where is he?"

"I think that's him over there," Iris muttered, pointing toward the hot dog stand. "You can just about see his tail poking out of that trash can."

"He's a dog again!" Evie beamed at the three girls. "That means the magic must have worn off." She looked around her. "I don't see the cart, so I'm guessing it's turned back into a potato, right?"

Iris didn't answer. She was looking at the twins who were looking at Evie.

"I think she must have bumped her head," one of them whispered. "She's talking such nonsense."

Her sister snorted. "Or maybe she just always talks like that."

They both sniggered.

Why are they being so mean? Evie wondered. *I know I squashed their sandcastles, but it was an accident.* She tried to force a smile onto her face. *Come on, Wonder Waitress, pretend they're just cranky customers in the café, because you're good at dealing with them, like that woman in the white pants who you spilled the cherry pancakes all over! (FACT: White pants and cherry sauce don't mix.) But once you explained that you were just learning, it turned out she used to be a waitress, too, and then she was kind and gave you loads of advice and left you a really big tip!*

"I'm so sorry," Evie said, scrambling out of the crushed remains of their sand structure. "I really couldn't control the cart. I've never driven one before. But I'll help you rebuild." She grabbed a bucket and began filling it with sand.

"Don't bother!" one of the twins said, tossing her blond hair and scowling at Evie. "It's too late!"

Her sister puffed out her cheeks. "I'm hot," she moaned to her twin. "Want to go get some ice cream? I could eat a bucket load."

Evie looked at the twins. *Ice cream? Bucket loads of ice cream?* In among the chaos of the crash, a tiny seed of an idea had somehow just blown into her head and now a big smile was washing over her face. "Oh my word!" she gasped. "You guys have just given me THE best idea for a new dessert. You see, my parents run a café near the boardwalk and we do the most amazing ice creams. And I've just thought of a new sundae that looks exactly like a sandcastle! See, we could serve it in a bucket with a little spoon shaped like a spade, just like this—" She held up the bucket and waggled it in front of them. "And then the customer could turn the dessert out onto their plate, like so—" She upended the bucket and revealed the sand-castle she'd made.

Evie's eyes sparkled. "I've even thought of a name for it: Sandcastle Sundaes! I'll make you both one to say sorry for squishing your sculpture. But first I have to go tell my stepmom. This could help us win the Best Café Contest!" She paused to catch her breath, while the twins just stared at her, their eyes wide, their mouths open. Then—

EVIE BROWN'S EASY SENSATIONAL SANDCASTLE SUNDAE RECIPE

This is a quick and easy vanilla ice cream recipe.

You will need:

- ½ cup and 5 tablespoons of sweetened condensed milk
- 2 ½ cups of double cream/heavy whipping cream
- 1 teaspoon of vanilla extract
- Plastic beakers (freezer-proof containers)
- Plastic wrap

Method:

- Put condensed milk, cream, and vanilla into an electric mixer and whisk until very thick. (You can do this by hand, but it will take lot of elbow grease!)

- Line plastic beakers with plastic wrap and freeze until set (4-6 hours).

*** * 🌙 * ***

"You're crazy!" one of the twins said. "Right, Clara?"

But her sister didn't reply. Clara was still staring at the sandcastle Evie had made, as though she was giving the idea a lot of thought. Then she snorted. "Katie-Belle's right. You're nuts!" And she snatched up the bucket and spade that Evie had used. "Come on," she called to her sister. "Let's go find Mom."

"Well, that went well," Iris said as she and Evie watched the twins march away. "But at least Agent C doesn't seem to have spotted us yet. Look, see that tiny dot down there by the water? That's her! I told her I might have seen a shoe over there, and she's gone to search for it, which gives us time to escape."

Evie didn't reply. She was watching the twins walking across the sand toward a blond woman who was sunbathing. "You know, I think I've seen those girls before." She kept her eyes on the twins as they crouched down next to their mom. She saw them pointing in her direction, and their mom turning and staring at Evie . . . "Oh no!" Evie gasped as her eyes locked with the mom's. "That's the lady I crashed into this morning."

"No way!" Iris winced. "That's Mrs. Pemberton. The Pembertons are one of the best-connected families in Lime Bay. They own loads of businesses. They've got this really fancy café and—"

"What?" Evie said. "They own a café? Then

why did they come to our diner this morning? Unless . . ." She looked back at the family. "Unless they were checking us out?"

Iris chuckled. "Sizing up the competition? Yep, that sounds like the Pembertons. Katie-Belle and Clara are SO competitive. At school they have to win everything, or they make such a fuss."

"Well, I guess they won't be saving me a place in the lunch line when school starts." Evie shrugged. "Maybe I'll find a way to make it up to them. But now I have to get back to the diner and tell Hannah about my new dessert idea. She'll love it. Hey, Fudge!" she shouted. "Here, boy!"

"But what about the Agents of H.E.A.R.T.?" Iris checked to make sure Agent C was still at the other end of the beach. "We've got to keep out of sight."

"Nah!" Evie smiled. "I like the agents. If Agent C hadn't turned Fudge into a donkey, I wouldn't have had my amazing dessert idea. And if I help my parents win the Best Café Contest, then maybe they'll let me keep Fudge!"

CHAPTER 10

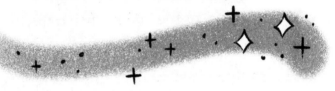

Evie felt about ten feet tall as they jogged back up the beach. She was having THE most exciting day—a real-life fairy tale adventure, with princesses and magic and yeah, a bit of mayhem . . . Plus, she had the cutest dog on the planet racing alongside her AND the best ice cream idea EVER. Not to mention a possible new buddy. She glanced across at Iris. *I really hope we will be friends. Lime Bay is WAY more fun since I met you.*

Iris noticed Evie smiling at her and grinned back. "So, do you really think your stepmom is going to let you keep Fudge?"

"Sure. My big cousin Dylan says the way to get parents to agree to stuff is to make sure you ask them when they're in their 'happy place.'"

"Um . . . where's that?" Iris asked.

Evie giggled. "It's not a place. It's a feeling. You have to ask them at the right time, when they're relaxed and happy. Dylan says that's how he got his mom to agree to his nose piercing."

"Whoa!" Iris's eyes widened. "That's so cool."

"Yeah, it's a tiny green emerald. It's awesome. And if I help Hannah win the Best Café Contest, then she'll be in her happy place and she'll be much more likely to let me keep Fudge."

"Hey—look!" Iris pointed to the café up ahead. "I think your stepmom's looking for you."

Hannah was outside, on the terrace, shielding her eyes from the sun, scanning the beach. "Evie! There you are!" she shouted. "Thank goodness. I was starting to get worried." Then she spotted the dog and her smile vanished. "Oh no, didn't you find its owner?"

Evie scooped up the pup and crossed the street. She raced up the steps to the terrace. "No, but I did have THE best idea for a new dessert. I can't wait to tell you about it." She held the pup tighter as he tried to scramble out of her arms. "No, Fudge! You can't go in there. I think he likes the diner." She beamed at her stepmom. But Hannah just sighed.

"Evie, I told you. He can't stay here. If the judge sees him, we'll never win the competition." She smiled at Iris, who had joined Evie on the terrace now.

"Oh, don't worry about the judges," Evie said. "My new dessert idea is going to knock their socks off! See, it's this ice cream that looks like a sand-castle. You serve it in a little bucket that the customer turns out onto their plate. I've even thought of a name for it: Sandcastle Sundaes and—"

"That's great, honey," Hannah interrupted. "But first we need to deal with the dog."

"Later, I promise!" Evie crossed her fingers under Fudge's paws and hoped that promises didn't really count when it came to super-cute homeless puppies. "But please can we make the dessert? The judge could come at any moment and—"

"Precisely!" Hannah put some dirty glasses from one of the tables onto her tray. "And if the judge sees a dog in the diner, no way will we win, and then—"

But the rest of her words were interrupted by a shout from the street below. "Iris! Have you borrowed my cell again?"

They all turned to see Iris's granny striding up the steps to the terrace, her flowery frock billowing in the breeze.

"Oh . . . um . . . Hi, Gammy." Iris's face turned tomato red. "I'm sorry I forgot to ask you first." She dug in her bag and pulled out the cell. "Here you go."

"Thank you," her granny said, taking it back. "But next time, check in with me first, okay? Someone might have been trying to order a bouquet. Hi, I'm Frankie Flowers," she added to Hannah, with a smile so wide it made her eyes crinkle, "which is a great name for a florist, right?" She laughed. "But most folks just call me Gammy on account of me having a whole soccer team of grandkids in this town."

"Nice to meet you. I'm Hannah Brown," Evie's stepmom said. "And this is Evie."

"And this is Fudge!" Evie added, as the pup tried to jump out of her arms to welcome Gammy.

"Who is just visiting and definitely NOT staying!" Hannah said firmly.

At that moment Fudge managed to wriggle free. He jumped down and dived for Gammy, wagging his tail, licking her hands, and fussing around her legs for attention.

"Oh hello, little fella." Gammy beamed. "He's adorable."

"That's what I keep telling Hannah," Evie said. "And he's homeless and he really wants to stay here; he'd make a brilliant guard dog."

"Really?" Hannah raised an eyebrow. "How? By licking intruders to bits?"

But Evie wasn't about to give up. "I'm sure he'd let us know if someone came into the yard. And he wouldn't cost you anything. I'd pay for all his food out of my allowance."

Hannah shook her head. "You know we can't keep him— Oh, I'm so sorry," she added, as Fudge jumped up at Gammy to give her another lick. "The dog turned up here this morning and we've no idea what to do with him."

"Shame we've got a cat," Gammy said, stroking Fudge's head so his tail began to wag even faster. "Or I'd be tempted to take him home."

"Puddles wouldn't mind," Iris said. "He's not scared of dogs."

"But I think the pup would be scared of Puddles!" Gammy chuckled. "Anyway, this little guy has probably got a perfectly good home, though he could do with a bath."

"I agree," Hannah said. "I just wish his owners would come find him."

"But he doesn't belong to anyone," Evie said. A bubble of frustration was growing in her belly. *Why isn't Hannah listening?*

"Well, if he is a stray, perhaps my friend Dawn could help," Gammy said. "She runs a pet shelter just down the street. I could take him there for you."

What? No way! Evie looked at Iris—her eyes wide. *I don't want to take Fudge to a pet shelter. We've got to stop this!*

Iris seemed to understand what Evie was trying to tell her. She coughed. "Um, I don't know, Gammy. The shelter's always very busy . . ."

"And what if Fudge's owners come looking for him here?" Evie added.

"Then we'll direct them to the shelter," Hannah said. "That's so kind of you," she added to Gammy. "Maybe the girls could go with you? I'm so busy today, it would be great if Evie had something to do."

Huh? Evie couldn't believe her ears. *I don't need to find something to do! I've got competition-winning ice creams to make. And besides, I am NOT handing Fudge over to some shelter.* "I really think me and Fudge should stay here," Evie said. "At least until the judge has come and—"

"No, Evie!" Hannah shook her head. "I'm sorry. But the dog is NOT staying! Thanks again for offering to take him to the shelter," she added to Gammy.

"No problem," Gammy said. "I'll just go ask Bryan to watch my stall. He has the souvenir stand next to mine. I'll be back in a moment."

As Gammy walked back down the steps, Hannah scanned the street in both directions. "Still no sign of that judge," she said. "I wish they'd hurry up. I feel so tense waiting for them."

"Which is why you need me here," Evie tried again.

Hannah frowned. "Oh, look! There's a customer waiting at the counter," she said, changing the subject. And she headed back inside.

"Urgh!" Evie collapsed onto one of the chairs and Fudge jumped up onto her lap, resting his head on her shoulder. "It's so annoying! I need to be here making the Sandcastle Sundae for the judge. Not dropping Fudge off at some animal shelter."

Iris sat down next to her and gave the pup a

stroke. "Your stepmom really doesn't like him, does she?"

"She might change her mind if I could help her win the contest." Evie sighed. "But how can I do that if I'm not here?"

"You might be back quicker than you think," Iris said. "The shelter really does get busy. A few weeks ago, we had to foster a few chickens for Dawn because it was full."

Evie nodded, but that sounded like a long shot. She hugged Fudge closer and buried her face in his warm fur. "I'm going to need a miracle if I want to keep you." Then suddenly an idea popped into her head. "Wait—maybe it's not a miracle I need—perhaps I just need some magic!" Her eyes sparkled as she leaped to her feet. "Quick! We need to go find Agent C. She says you can do ANYTHING with magic."

Iris rolled her eyes. "Yeah, like making lame coaches out of potatoes and turning dogs into donkeys and—"

"But that's exactly what I need! Maybe she can make Fudge invisible. Or tiny. Or turn him into a goldfish until Hannah gets used to the idea of me having a pet."

"I don't know . . ." Iris scratched her head. "Agent C isn't very reliable. She's more likely to turn him into a gorilla than a goldfish! And besides, you've seen her magic. It never lasts long."

"But we've got to do something," Evie said.

Just then, they heard a loud whistle from the street below.

The girls peered over the edge of the terrace.

"It's Agent R!" Evie said. "Maybe she can do magic, too?"

Iris grunted. "I don't think so—and hey, what's that long brown thing she's carrying?"

CHAPTER 11

"Evie!" Agent R shouted. "Look what I got you!" She hitched up her frock, flicked her silver hair over her shoulder, and charged toward them. "We're ditching the hair dye idea," she said, launching herself up onto the café terrace with one giant leap. "Because I got you this!"

Fudge let out an excited bark and strained to try to grab the long, hairy thing Agent R was dangling in front of her.

"Uh-oh," Iris whispered. "My big cousin Anna has a wig like that, and it itched like crazy."

"It's not a wig!" Agent R snapped. "It's a hair extension."

"Whoa! It's as tall as me," Evie said, peering at the hairpiece that Agent R was holding out in front of her now like a sports banner.

"You'll love it," Agent R said. "Look, it gets stuck on like this." And she grabbed the end of the hairpiece, pulled off a sticky tab, then patted the extension onto the back of Evie's short bob. "Fitted with fairy tale gum," she said with a wink. "Guaranteed to last forever."

"Forever?" Evie reached one hand behind and tried to tug the thing off. "Hey—it's stuck!"

"Of course it's stuck," Agent R said. "It wouldn't be much use to you if it fell off. Duh!" She rolled her eyes. "Now all we need to do is a bit of styling." She

flipped around a belt
bag that was tied to
her waist and pulled out
a comb. "If you don't absolutely love it, I'll chop it off.
Deal?" But she didn't wait for
an answer. She picked up the hairpiece and began
twisting and turning it into a braid.

Evie sucked in her cheeks. "That hurts!"

"Oh, quit complaining!" Agent R said, pulling
the hair even tighter. "You can't bake a cake if you
don't break some eggs!"

"My big cousin Anna is exactly the same," Iris whispered to Evie. "She works at the salon and she's a super-mean hairstyling machine."

"Zip it, Miss Chatty!" Agent R said, shooting a scowl at Iris. "Or you're next! And you!" she added, glaring at Fudge, who was wriggling to get down from Evie's arms again.

"Okay—ENOUGH!" Evie stamped her foot and turned to glare at Agent R. "STOP TUGGING MY HAIR!" At the sound of Evie's loud voice, Fudge dived out of her arms and hid under a table. "Oops—sorry, little guy," Evie said. "I wasn't shouting at you."

"All done!" Agent R said, securing the end with a silver hair elastic that she pulled off her wrist. "Now, tell me you don't love it?"

Evie reached behind her head and felt the thick braid. "It's kind of heavy."

Agent R snorted. "If it wasn't heavy, and thick and long and super strong, you'd never be able to use it as an escape rope when your wicked stepmom locks you in the tower. As I always say, *'If there's no stair, just use your hair!'"*

"But I keep telling you," Evie said, picking up the end of the braid so she wouldn't stand on it. "Hannah would never lock me in a tower."

"That's what they all say. Then suddenly it's: clunk, clank, clink!" Agent R said, miming locking a door. "And next thing you know, you're a prisoner in a big brick jail." She stepped back and stared at Evie's hair. "Mmm, there's something missing."

"A pair of scissors to chop it off?" Iris suggested.

"Hilarious!" Agent R said. "I know what it is. You need a tiara."

"I really don't," Evie said. "See, I had to wear one to my parents' wedding. It felt like my head was stuck in a bucket of crabs: so tight and nippy and scratchy and—"

"You NEED a tiara," Agent R interrupted, "so that you can bend it into a key to escape from the tower."

"But I keep telling you, I am NOT going to get locked in a tower."

"Whatever!" Agent R puffed out her cheeks. "So, which way to the tiara shop?"

"There isn't one in Lime Bay," Iris said.

Thank goodness! Evie thought. *Now I need to find out if you can do magic spells like Agent C . . .* But before Evie could ask her—

"Okay. I'll just have to make a tiara myself," Agent R said. "Go fetch me a wire coat hanger," she told Evie. "And maybe some metal forks or screwdrivers . . . I'll bend them into shape." And she flexed her bicep to show just how strong she was.

AGENT R'S GUIDE ON HOW TO MAKE A TIARA (NO SCREWDRIVERS NECESSARY!)

Note: Unless you're an actual, real, fist-pumping, muscle-flexing Secret Agent from H.E.A.R.T., then please use pipe cleaners, not screwdrivers! —Agent R

You will need:

- Pipe cleaners (sparkly ones work best)
- Crafty materials for decoration

Method:

- Bend and twist your favorite color of pipe cleaners into the shape of your head.

- Or use a hairband and attach your twisted pipe cleaner shapes to it.

- Use more pipe cleaners to create this design with shapes such as hearts, stars, triangles, loops, etc., which you can twist onto your base.

- Try threading beads and ribbons into your design.

Evie gasped. A tiara made from a coat hanger and cutlery and screwdrivers sounded even more scratchy and painful than the one she had worn to the wedding! "Um . . . what about that tiara shop out of town?" Evie said, staring at Iris with huge eyes, hoping she'd pick up on her plan.

"Huh?" Iris looked confused; then she suddenly noticed Evie's pleading look. "Oh . . . er, yeah, sure, THAT tiara shop."

"Well? Where is it?" Agent R said.

"Just follow the street out of town . . ." Evie pointed vaguely off into the distance. "Then keep going and going, and you can't miss it."

"That's right," Iris said, joining in now. "It's about ten miles out of town. It's called Tiaras-R-Us, and it sells the most amazing ones you've ever seen—pink, purple, rainbow-colored!"

Agent R nodded. "Ten miles, you say?"

"Sure, you might want to take the bus," Evie suggested.

"Nah!" Agent R did a few leg bends and lunges,

then stretched out her hamstrings. "Rescue agents don't take buses. We run! Fast!" She pulled up the hem of her dress to reveal a pair of sporty satin trainers. "Agent C is the only one who wears silly shoes. Right, back soon!"

"Wait!" Evie cried. "Before you go, there's something I need to ask you . . . Can you do magic, like Agent C? Because if you can, maybe you can use it to help me keep Fudge."

Agent R snorted, then pointed to her bicep. "I use muscle; not magic! But, hey, he could be useful." She bent down to Fudge and did a quick measurement around his neck with her hands. "I'll make him a collar that matches your tiara and we'll put a tiny pair of wire cutters in a little pouch, which we can hang from it. Then you'll be able to cut your way through the bars on your tower window. Neat idea, huh? Now, I gotta go. See ya!" With one giant leap she hit the street and then charged off, her silver hair spreading out behind her like a shiny, superhero cape.

"But wait—" Evie shouted after her. "You said you'd cut this braid off if I didn't like it. And I don't!"

Just then they heard a gasp from the diner door.

"Oh my word!" Hannah cried, nearly dropping the tray she was carrying. "What on earth have you done to your hair?"

CHAPTER 12

Evie gazed at her stepmom's shocked face, desperately trying to think of a way to explain how and why she had somehow morphed into Rapunzel in the five minutes while she'd been away. *Maybe I should just tell her the truth, that I'm being helped by three fairy tale friends who think I need rescuing from her!*

"It's dress-up!" Iris blurted out.

"Really?" Hannah cocked her head to one side.

"Um, sure," Iris said, her face turning pink. "All the kids in Lime Bay like to do dress-up. It's a thing here." She fumbled in her bag and pulled out her old floppy hat and dark glasses and shoved them on. "Ta-da!"

Hannah still didn't look convinced. In fact, she looked, to Evie, like she was about to ask a whole box of awkward questions, when they heard a shout from the street.

"Are you girls ready?" Gammy was waiting at the bottom of the terrace steps. "Oh, goodness!" she said, doing a double take. "I like your hair, Evie . . . It's . . . um . . . very dramatic." She put on the purple eyeglasses that hung on a chain around her neck to get a better look. "Is that your cousin Anna's wig?" she asked Iris. "I hope you checked with her before you borrowed it this time."

"Oh . . . er." Iris looked a little squirmy about her fib now. "Is it time to go?" she asked, changing the subject.

But I don't want to go! Evie looked around and wondered whether it was worth making a run for it with Fudge. *But where could we hide?* Reluctantly she slowly gathered up her braid AND Fudge and followed Iris down the steps onto the street, trying not to trip on her hair.

"Bye, and thanks again," Hannah called to Gammy.

"Wait—are you sure he can't stay?" Evie turned back to her stepmom, with her most pleading look, but she was drowned out by Fudge, who had started barking loudly at a dog on the other side of the street. He tried to wriggle free to get to it.

"No, Fudge!" Evie said, holding him tighter. "You can't just run off when we're on the street. You might have an accident."

"Don't worry about that," Gammy said. "Look what my friend Bryan loaned me." She held out a bright red collar and leash.

"That's Monty's!" Iris grinned. "He's Bryan's dog," she added to Evie. "He's huge! I think he might actually be half horse."

"Luckily Bryan always keeps a spare," Gammy said. "Here, try it on the pup."

"He doesn't seem to like it much." Iris giggled as Evie slipped the collar over Fudge's head. "Looks like he's trying to push it off with his paws."

"That's exactly what you're like when I suggest you wear a dress, Iris!" Gammy smiled. "Come on now, let's take him to the shelter."

Not if I can help it, Evie thought. *There's got to be a way to get out of this: Where is Agent C and her magic wand when I need her?*

"So how are you enjoying Lime Bay?" Gammy asked Evie as they walked along the street.

"Er . . . well . . . it looks fun," Evie said, glancing around at the unfamiliar stores and people they were passing. In the three weeks since they'd moved to Lime Bay, her parents had been WAY too busy to explore the town properly. And the most Evie had seen of it was when she bounced extra high on her trampoline in the backyard at the diner. "I guess I don't know many people yet," she added as a group of older kids walked past, staring at her crazy hair.

"Don't worry. I can introduce you to everyone," Iris said. "The Flowers Family have lived here *forever*. Maybe I could give you a tour?"

Evie's eyes sparkled. "Oh yeah, let's do that now!" *And then maybe by the time we reach the shelter, it'll be full!*

"Well, I don't think we've got time for that," Gammy said. "But there's plenty to look at on the way."

"Like loads of my relatives' stores!" Iris giggled. "See, that's the problem with Lime Bay. There's always a family member keeping their beady eyes on me!"

"Iris!" Gammy chuckled.

"It's true. We did a Lime Bay family tree project at school and I filled an entire wall of the classroom."

Iris Flowers's Family Tree

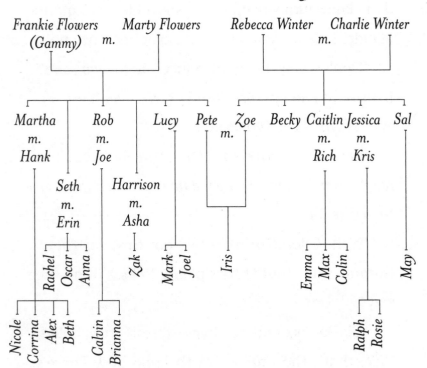

Evie's eyes goggled. She was an only child, with just three cousins!

Evie Brown's Family Tree

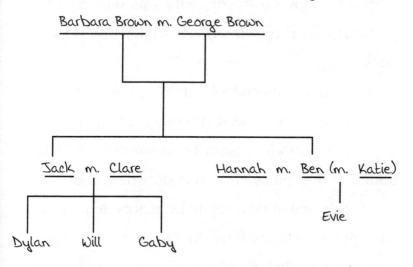

"Wow! I'd love to hear more about Lime Bay AND your family," Evie said, slowing down now to the pace of an extremely tired snail. "And please, take your time. I'm not in a rush at all."

"Well, for starters, my mom and dad don't always live in Lime Bay," Iris said. "They're musicians; they're away on tour a lot, so I mostly live with Gammy. But look—" She pointed to a poster in the window of a music shop they were passing. "They'll be playing at the Lime Bay Festival soon— Oh, hey, Uncle Hank." She waved to a man with a long, droopy mustache, who was dusting the guitars in the shop window. He smiled and waved back.

Evie tried to linger, looking in the store window, but Iris and Gammy were already moving on.

"And my mom's cousin Trina works here," Iris added as they passed the craft store next door.

"Is this one of your relatives' places, too?" Evie said, pointing to the fancy-looking café next door. Its tables outside had thick, white cloths and fussy flower arrangements.

"No, that's the Pembertons' place," Iris whispered.

Evie watched as a smartly dressed waiter came out carrying four complicated-looking desserts to one of the tables. *Whoa!* she thought, *it's going to be*

hard to beat the Pembertons in the Best Café Contest;
their place is so posh!

Just at that moment, Clara and Katie-Belle and their mom appeared from the beach side of the street—the girls still carrying their buckets and spades. The twins glared at Evie as they crossed in front of her, heading into the café. "Nice hair!" Evie heard one of them mutter, and the other laughed.

Evie puffed out her cheeks. "They really don't like me."

"They don't like anyone except themselves," Iris said.

"That's not kind." Gammy tried to look serious for a moment. "I'm sure the twins just—" She stopped talking and listened. "What's that noise? It sounds like the hundred and one dalmatians have come to town!"

Evie listened to the distant barking. Fudge gave a whimper and crept behind her legs.

"It must be coming from the pet shelter," Iris said. "It's just around the corner."

Gammy suddenly looked worried. "I hope Dawn's okay. She's been run off her feet since Hector retired."

As they turned onto the next street, the sound of the barking grew louder.

Iris pointed out a bookstore. "That's my aunt and uncle's place," she said, her voice louder now to be heard over the noise. "My cousin Zak is always in there. He's allergic to fresh air."

"Iris!" Gammy looked like she was trying not to laugh. "Zak just likes helping out."

"Well, if helping out means sitting in a big old comfy chair with his feet up, reading books all day, then yep, Zak is definitely the most helpful person in Lime Bay."

Gammy's reply was drowned out by the sudden sound of a dog howling like a wolf from a building across the street, followed by even louder barking.

"It's definitely coming from the shelter," Iris shouted.

"Oh dear, we'd better go see what's wrong," Gammy said. "Come on!"

But as Gammy and Iris went to cross the street, Evie hung back. Fudge was straining on the leash to get away from the noise. Evie bent down and scooped him up. "Don't worry. I'm not planning on taking you there," she whispered. *Think, Evie. Come on! There must be some way to avoid this.* She looked around desperately for an escape route, and spotted a display of books about Lime Bay in the bookstore window. "Wait," she called, to Iris and Gammy. "Um . . . before we go to the shelter, do you think we could pop into the bookstore? See, it's Dad's birthday next week, and we've been so busy at the diner I haven't had time to find him a gift. But I'm sure he'd love one of those books about Lime Bay." Evie felt Iris's eyes boring into hers. *Uh-oh! She knows I'm fibbing. Only it's not a fib,* Evie reminded herself. *Not completely.* It really was her dad's birthday next week.

Iris winked at her, then turned to Gammy. "Can we go see Zak first?" she shouted above the barking from across the street. "He'd love to meet Fudge. He's dog crazy!"

Gammy had her hands over her ears now. She nodded. "So long as your stepmom won't mind, Evie?"

She shook her head.

"Okay. But only ten minutes," Gammy said. "I'll go and see what's happening at the shelter. Here," she added, handing Iris her cell. "Call Dawn when you're ready to leave—the number is in my contacts. I'll come get you when you're done."

CHAPTER 13

"Neat trick," Iris whispered as they walked through the bookstore doors.

Evie felt her face grow hot. "It wasn't really a trick," she muttered. "It really is Dad's birthday next week . . . Oh wow!" she added, gazing around her. "This place is awesome."

They were in a long, tall, curving corridor, lined from floor to ceiling with bookshelves. Titles on every topic you could think of were stuffed into the groaning spaces.

"Zak claims the books are arranged alphabetically by subject," Iris said. "But it's not true, they're all in a muddle. See, Uncle Harrison and Aunt Asha don't mind if people come in and browse for hours. Sometimes I think people even sleep here! I guess when the customers get tired, they just put the books back where they feel like it."

They followed the corridor of books until it opened into a large high-ceilinged room that had a spiral staircase in the center, leading up to a balcony. All around them were little alcoves of books. *Like giant cubbyholes*, Evie thought. *This would be a great place for hide and seek!* "Hey—I bet even the Agents of H.E.A.R.T. couldn't find us here."

"I don't know. When they were bothering me, they even turned up in the deep end of the swimming pool. You should have seen their sparkly bathing suits!—Oh hi, Uncle Harrison!" Iris suddenly waved to a dark-haired man sitting behind a desk at the far end of the room. "Is it okay to bring my friend's dog in here? Oh wait, I think he's on the phone." The man smiled and waved back but carried on with his call. "I'm not sure if he saw Fudge, but I guess it's okay. Come on, we'll look for Zak."

"Is your aunt not here?" Evie glanced up to the balcony where there were even more books.

"Nah, she's probably out at a sale or something," Iris said. "Aunt Asha is the one who buys the books. Let me show you around . . . So, up there," she said pointing to the balcony, "is where they keep the brand-new books. And everything down here is second-hand, which is usually where Zak hangs out." She poked her head into the first alcove. "Zak, are you there? . . . Nope, no annoying bookworms in here."

For the next few minutes the girls and Fudge explored the ground floor of the bookstore, ducking into alcoves and nooks and crannies, checking behind giant stacks of old books that were taller than Evie, and exploring the little passageways that connected the different sections. But there was no sign of Zak anywhere.

"Maybe he's not here?" Evie said.

"Nah, he'll be hanging around somewhere. He's supposed to help customers to earn his allowance. But he's way too lazy. Isn't that right, Zak?" she said in a loud voice.

But if he was there, he didn't take the bait.

"It's like a rabbit burrow," Evie said, looking around yet another compartment stuffed full of dusty titles. "And I love the squishy cushions!" She dropped down onto one and Fudge launched himself onto her knee and licked her face. "Aw, do you like it here, too?" She tickled his ears, then glanced around at the shelves. There were so many old books. They reminded Evie of something . . . "Hey, Iris . . . I was wondering, where did you say the book of fairy tales came from? Before you had it, I mean."

Iris shrugged. "It just turned up in Gammy's bag. She couldn't remember where she'd found it."

"Well, I was thinking . . . What if it came from here? It would fit right in."

"Yeah, I guess . . . Shame Zak's not around," she added in a louder voice in case her cousin was listening. "Because he claims to know every book in the store!"

But if Zak was eavesdropping, he still didn't reply.

Iris bent down to look at a giant pile of stacked titles at the back of the room. "There sure are some strange books in here. Come and look at these; some of them are older than Gammy!"

Evie put Fudge down and went to see. She peered at the names on the spines. "*Miss Broom's Book of Household Charms*," she read aloud.

"*Tabitha West's Tales of Wizardry*," Iris added.

"*Conjuring for Cooks*!" Evie laughed. "My dad could do with that one at the diner."

Just then they heard a muffled sneeze.

The girls froze. Fudge gave a woof, then launched himself at the wall of books.

"Watch it!" Iris shouted. "They're going to fall!"

CHAPTER 14

Too late! The entire wall wobbled, then toppled, and then—CRASH!

As the books hit the ground, a figure with short dark hair and a bright red T-shirt, leaped out from behind. "Hey!" he gasped. "What do you think you're doing? You could have crushed me to death!" Then he caught sight of Fudge and his eyes sparkled.

"Zak!" Iris glared at her cousin. "I might have

known you'd be lurking somewhere. Why didn't you say hi? You must have heard us looking for you."

He shrugged. "I was busy—whoa!" He chuckled as Fudge hurled himself at him, wagging his tail and licking Zak all over. "Hi, fella, where did you come from?"

"You were busy doing what?" Iris interrupted. "Lounging about with a book?"

"Yep, reading, which is why I smash you in every school quiz." Zak looked up from fussing with Fudge and gave her a smug smile.

"That's not true!" Iris's face turned red. "And anyway, everyone knows I'm WAY better at sports than you. Even my cat Puddles is a better pitcher than you are."

"Is not!" Zak snapped.

"Is too!" Iris snapped back.

"Um . . . guys?" Evie said, but they were both too busy glaring at each other to notice. "Hi, I'm Evie Brown," she tried again, waving her hand in front of Zak's face. "And this is Fudge," she added. "We wanted to ask you about a book."

Zak looked at her; then did a double take. "Whoa! Hair!" he muttered, staring at her long braid.

"Oh yeah, this . . ." Evie tapped the long braid, wound around her arm. "I'd kind of forgotten about it. But see, this is kind of what we wanted to talk to you about."

"Well, I'm WAY too busy." Zak bent down and began rebuilding the wall of books.

"Here, let me help you." Evie crouched down and picked up a few titles. "See, we have this weird book, and we think it might have come from here."

Zak didn't say anything.

"It's sort of a magical book of fairy tales," Evie tried again.

He still didn't respond.

Evie pressed on anyway. "I made a wish when I was holding the book, and then these three princesses from the book came alive and offered to solve my problems, only they sometimes make a mess of things—hey, don't laugh, it's true!"

Zak rolled his eyes. "Fairy tale princesses coming alive and solving your problems? Right, like that could happen." He started stacking the books again.

"They did!" Evie glared at him. "It was the agents who gave me this crazy hair. And Fudge, here, too, which is actually quite awesome. But one of them wants to send me home in a potato carriage."

"Very funny," Zak muttered. "Like anyone would believe that—can you move your foot, you're standing on a book."

"Oh, sorry." Evie shuffled backward so he could retrieve the title and add it to his pile.

"Come on, Evie," Iris said. "Zak's obviously way too busy to help."

But Evie wasn't ready to leave. If they left the bookstore, there was only one place they could go— the pet shelter! "Maybe we could just show you the book," Evie began. But then something on the floor caught her eye. "Hey, wait—look at this." She picked up another book and held it up for Iris and Zak to see. "Do all the titles here have barcode stickers like this one?"

Zak nodded.

Evie showed Iris. "See the little black lines on the sticker. Some of the candy bars in the diner have barcodes, too. And when Hannah scans them she can check all sorts of things like where the candy came from and when it arrived at the diner. I'm guessing the barcodes here tell you the same thing. So maybe the book of fairy tales has a barcode, too."

"It doesn't," Zak said. "I checked when I found it—" As soon as he realized what he'd said, his hand shot up to cover his mouth, as though he was trying to stuff the words back in.

But it was too late. Iris's eyes flashed. "You mean you knew about the book all along? Then why didn't you say so?"

"I . . . um . . . well." Zak's face had turned red.

"Wait a minute . . ." Iris stared at her cousin, her eyes narrowing. "Don't tell me you had a visit from the Agents of H.E.A.R.T., too?"

"So what if I did!" Zak folded his arms. "It's none of your business."

Evie sighed. "I guess not everyone likes to be bothered by a bunch of strange princesses in frilly frocks."

"Exactly!" Zak said. "If you must know, I was trying to get my parents to let me have a pet mouse. I made a wish for one. Next thing I knew, the agents appeared. Only they thought I said 'spouse' not 'mouse.'"

"What's a spouse?" Iris asked.

Zak swallowed a few times and scuffed a bump in the carpet with the toe of his sneaker. "It's a partner, like a husband or a wife—hey, stop laughing, Iris!" He glared at her, and then he sighed. "The Agents of H.E.A.R.T. got it in their heads that I wanted to find someone to marry." He shuddered. "They said I'd have to learn to ride a horse first."

"Zak's scared of horses," Iris whispered to Evie. "A palomino pony bit him on the hand at summer camp last year."

"That's not the worst part," Zak said. "The grumpy agent, the one with the long silver hair, dangled me out of my bedroom window by my ankles and told me to climb back up the wall, in case I ever had to rescue someone trapped in a tower."

"Terrifying!" Evie said.

"And don't even mention the outfit the one in the pink dress made me wear." Zak shuddered again. "It was hideous."

"Tights and a frilly shirt?" Evie suggested. She'd seen loads of handsome princes in fairy tale books and they always seemed to wear the same sort of clothes.

"Those tights were so itchy!" Zak hung his head.

"*Sheesh!* And I thought I had it bad with the braid," Evie said.

"Hold on . . ." Iris frowned. "I bet it was you who dumped the book in Gammy's bag, so you could get rid of the agents through me."

Zak flushed again.

"I knew it!" Iris scowled at him. "So, it was your fault I ended up at ball practice wearing a big fancy frock!"

"Um, wait up," Evie interrupted. "That whole book-dump thing . . . that's kind of what you did to me."

Iris looked at her, then back at her cousin, and then her scowl slowly disappeared. "I guess that's true."

"Pax?" Zak said, holding up his hand.

Iris nodded. "Okay, pax!"

"Huh?" Evie looked confused.

"It's Latin for 'peace,'" Zak explained. "Gammy makes us say it when we've been arguing. So, the book . . . have you still got it?"

Iris opened her bag and pulled it out.

Zak flicked through the pages, and Evie noticed his hands were shaking. *I guess he really doesn't want to have to wear those tights again!*

"Let me show you something," he said, holding out a page to her and Iris. "See, this is where Cinderella, or Agent C, appears at the ball. She's supposed to be in the illustration, right? But—"

"She's just a silhouette?" Evie said.

Zak nodded. "When the agents are here, their pictures vanish from their stories."

"Wow!" Iris said. "I didn't notice that before."

Zak turned a few more pages. "There's something else. See, there are loads of different stories." He began to read the list aloud. "Cinderella, Beauty and the Beast, Rapunzel, Sleeping Beauty, Little Red Riding Hood—"

Evie's eyes goggled. "Are you saying you think the characters from those stories could jump out of the book, too?"

"Hey—maybe this explains why we had different agents visiting us," Iris said. "We both met Agent C and Agent R, right? But I never met Beauty."

Zak frowned. "I saw Agent C and Agent R. But they had another one with them—Agent F."

"Who? Wait—let me guess." Iris peered at the list of stories, and then a smile spread over her face. "The Princess and the Frog!" She burst out laughing. "Was she hoping to turn you into a prince with one smacker?"

Zak glared at her.

"Pax, remember!" Evie said. "Come on, Zak, what were you saying?"

He shrugged. "Just that, yes, there may be more characters who can escape from the book. And then there's the baddies. If the good characters can get out, maybe the bad ones can, too."

"What?" Evie blinked at him. "You mean the wicked stepmom? The mean witch? The big bad wolf?"

"For the record, you're more likely to be killed by a lightning strike than a wolf," Zak said, bending down to tickle Fudge's ears. "I bet you knew that, didn't you, boy, because you're related to them, aren't you. Wolves are really shy creatures," he added. "I've got a book about them somewhere . . ." He looked around as if he were searching for it.

 ## ZAK FLOWERS'S FAVORITE FACTS ABOUT WOLVES

- Wolves howl to communicate.

- Their feet measure around 4 inches wide by 5 inches long.

- The average length of a wolf is around 6 feet, nose to tail.

- Wolves rarely attack humans.

- Their sprinting speed is 36-38 mph.

- Adult wolves have 42 teeth.

- Wolves often mate for life.

- Wolves live in packs, usually around 6-8 animals, but there can be smaller or larger packs with extended family members.

- A wolf pack has structure and rules and is led by an alpha male and female.

- All wolves in the pack help raise the young.

Sources of wolf facts: National Geographic, nationalgeographic. com; wolfmatters.org; the International Wolf Center, wolf.org; National Wildlife Federation, nwf.org; Living with Wolves, livingwithwolves.org

But just then, there was a beeping sound from Iris's bag.

"Gammy's cell!" Iris rummaged in her bag and pulled it out. "Hello? Oh hi, Gammy—" She was quiet for a moment, listening, then—"What?" Iris's eyes widened. "No way!" She looked at Zak and Evie. "Sure! We'll come help you right away." She ended the call and picked up her bag. "Guys, we've got to go to the pet shelter; it's an emergency! Gammy says all the cages are open and the animals are escaping!"

CHAPTER 15

In less than two minutes Zak had told his dad where they were going, and the three of them—plus Fudge—raced across the street, where Gammy was waiting for them by the shelter gate.

"Oh, thank goodness!" she cried, over the noise of barking. "It's chaos in here."

Fudge strained to run away, but Evie scooped him up. "Don't worry, boy," she whispered. "I'm not going to leave you here. But we've got to help the other animals." She followed Zak and Iris inside. Dogs! Ducks! Cats! Guinea pigs! Creatures of every shape and size were spilling out of pens, barking and meowing and clucking and racing and chasing around the yard. A brown Shetland pony whinnied and swished its tail as several cats had a standoff between its feet, hissing and spitting at one another. And right in the middle was an older lady with curly gray hair and a bright red face, who was trying to gather them all up.

"Hi," she called to them. "I'm Dawn," she added, to Evie. "Thanks for coming. Can you help us?"

"But what's going on?" Zak asked, reaching down to trap a rabbit that was trying to escape through the open door behind them.

"We've no idea," Dawn said, taking the rabbit from him. "All the pens just keep popping open."

Evie gazed around the yard. Nearly every cage that lined the sides of the shelter's outside space was empty—the doors wide open. And then suddenly she saw what was happening. "Agent B!"

Iris and Zak had spotted her, too. Beauty was squatting in front of a pen at the far end, unhooking the bolt.

Zak's face had turned pale. He took a step backward, glancing around. "Are the other agents here, too?"

"I don't know. I only see Beauty." Evie tied Fudge's leash to a hook on the wall behind them, then gathered up her braid. "Quick, we need to stop her."

"Um . . . okay, I guess," Zak muttered, taking another step backward.

Iris chuckled. "Don't worry, cuz, if she tries to make you wear itchy tights, I promise I'll protect you!"

"Very funny!" Zak glared at her.

"Guys!" Evie said. "Beauty's letting those guinea pigs out. Come on!"

They raced over, leaving Gammy and Dawn to

separate a group of dogs who were rolling around in a big ball of wriggly legs, heads, and tails.

"Beauty! What are you doing?" Evie cried.

Agent B peeped out from behind her thick bangs. "Oh hi, Evie! Hi, everyone," she added, smiling at Iris—and Zak, who was hanging back a little, trying not to be noticed. "I'm looking for Fancy Pants, your tabby cat. Remember? You told me he was missing. You must be so sad without him." She reached up and patted Evie on the hand. "But don't worry. I shall find him for you. Because as I always say, a home isn't a home without lots of beasts of one's own!"

Evie groaned. *Oh no, this is all my fault.*

"Um, who is Fancy Pants?" Zak whispered.

"It's a long story," Iris muttered.

Agent B let out a sigh. "Oh dear, these guinea pigs tell me they don't know Fancy Pants, either. I've been asking all the creatures in here, but unfortunately, no one seems to have heard of your cat, Evie. But there are still a few more to try . . ." She

shuffled along to the next pen, unhooked the bolt, and poked her head inside, making strange snuffling sounds to the rabbits sitting there.

Evie looked at Iris. "If only I hadn't fibbed," she whispered.

"About what?" Zak frowned. "I don't understand."

"Well, I kind of told Agent B that I'd lost our cat," Evie whispered. "Only we don't have a cat."

Zak grinned. "Ah, I get it. You were trying to get rid of her, right?"

Evie nodded.

"Don't worry," Iris said. "Just point to any old cat and tell her it belongs to you— Look! What about that one over there," she added, pointing to a large black cat stalking past. "That could be your cat?"

"Or this one," Zak added, as a ginger kitty jumped up on top of the pen next to him. Zak reached over and stroked its ears. "Yeah, definitely this one. It's so friendly."

Evie shook her head. "I can't take a cat home, as well as Fudge. What would Hannah say? She's my stepmom," Evie added for Zak's benefit.

Agent B stood up and dusted down her frock. "I'm so sorry, Evie. The rabbits don't know any cat called Fancy Pants, either. But they've promised to help look for him, along with all your other friends in here. Isn't it wonderful that they're all searching for your cat?"

Evie glanced around at the chaos of the yard. *So THAT'S why Beauty is releasing all the animals—to help me find my nonexistent pet.* Evie felt a wobble of guilt in her belly. *Somehow, I've got to tell Agent B the truth—and fast!* She took a deep breath. "It's so kind of you to look for Fancy Pants, only the problem is, I sort of made him up. It was a story—"

"I LOVE stories!" Agent B clapped her hands in delight. "And so do animals. I often take a book into the enchanted forest and read aloud to the creatures there. Did I tell you I used to run a mobile library, just for animals? You simply must read to

Fudge—and Fancy Pants—whenever you can, Evie. Animals have such wonderful imaginations. Oh, look—chickens!" she said, pointing to another pen. "They're very chatty. If Fancy Pants has been here, they will definitely know." And with that she swept off toward their enclosure.

BEAUTY'S FAVORITE BOOKS TO READ ALOUD TO BEASTS

Beauty loves to read to beasts, and she'd love you to try it, too! These are some of her favorite stories:

- *Aesop's Fables*

- *The Bear and the Piano* by David Litchfield

- *Can I Be Your Dog?* by Troy Cummings

- *A Cat's Christmas Carol* by Sam Hay and Helen Shoesmith

- *How the Leopard Got His Claws* by Chinua Achebe

- *Lost and Found* by Oliver Jeffers

- "The Owl and the Pussy-Cat" by Edward Lear

- *Rice & Rocks* by Sandra L. Richards

- *The Sheep-Pig* by Dick King-Smith

- *Skippyjon Jones* by Judy Schachner

- *Smelly Louie* by Catherine Rayner

- *The Snail and the Whale* by Julia Donaldson and Axel Scheffler

- *The Squirrels Who Squabbled* by Rachel Bright and Jim Field

- *The Tale of Mrs. Tiggy-Winkle* by Beatrix Potter

- *The Very Hungry Caterpillar* by Eric Carle

- *The Wind in the Willows* by Kenneth Grahame

✳ ∘˙∘ ◇ ✳˙∘ ◇✳ ∘˙∘ ◇ ✳

"Shall I go football tackle her?" Iris offered. "I think I could bring her down with one jump, then we could maybe sit on her?"

"What? No! This isn't Agent B's fault." Evie sighed and scratched at her braid, which was feeling uncomfortably heavy now. "I just need to get her attention and explain everything to her."

"That never works!" Iris folded her arms. "You can holler as much as you like, but once the agents are on a mission they won't pay any attention."

Zak nodded. "Agent R refused to stop dangling me out of my bedroom window no matter how much I yelled at her."

"Well, perhaps we can distract her," Evie said.

"Like the little boy in the diner this morning. He was mad because we'd run out of gummy bears, but then I showed him how to make a Pup Cone and fold a dog napkin and—"

"Huh? Back up a bit there . . . What diner?" Zak interrupted. "And what do you mean you ran out of gummy bears? And hey—why were you folding dog napkins?"

"Later!" Iris told him. "But Evie, we don't have any napkins." Her eyes were on Agent B, who was inside the chicken coop now.

"We do have loads of dogs, though." Evie was gazing at an extra-friendly-looking large dog that was bounding past them. "Hey! Agent B!" she called to Beauty. "What sort of puppy is that?"

Beauty turned to look.

"Here, boy," Evie shouted. "Come and say hi to my friend Beauty—whoa!" She laughed as the dog nearly knocked her over with his giant waggly tail. Then he grabbed hold of the end of her long braid and gave it a playful chew. "Hey—let go!" Evie giggled. "Wait! On second thought, keep chewing. Chew it right off!" But the dog had let go of Evie's hair and was diving toward Agent B.

"Oh, what a gem!" Beauty said, stepping out of the chicken pen to hug him. "A big dribbly-wibbly, hairy hug-box! I could go *mutts* over you," she breathed.

"'A hairy hug-box'?" Zak mouthed. "Sheesh!"

Iris giggled. Evie tried not to join in, but it was hard to keep her face straight. "So, er . . . do you think he's some sort of greyhound, maybe?" she asked Agent B.

"Oh, no, no, no, Evie—he's far too shaggy," Agent B said. "His paws are too big. His head is too wide. And that tail! Let me tell you about the character-istics of the greyhound . . ."

And while she chatted away and fussed over the dog, Evie and Iris tiptoed over and caught some escaping chickens and fastened the bolt on the coop. Meanwhile Zak quietly picked up one of the rabbits that had hopped out and returned it safely to its pen. They were just signaling to one another to go help Gammy and Dawn with the other animals, when—

"Oh, Evie, great news!" Agent B suddenly cried. "This lovely dog has been telling me about a row of trash cans on the other side of town where many cats like to gather for a chat. Perhaps that's where Fancy Pants is!"

"Oh, um . . . that's kind of you, only, there is no Fancy Pants," Evie began. "I made him up when you and the other agents were arguing and—"

But Agent B was already striding toward the gate. "Have no fear, Evie, I shall bring back your cat!"

CHAPTER 16

E vie groaned. "This is a total disaster."

"Well, at least it keeps her out of your *hair* for a while," Zak said, grinning at Evie's giant braid.

"But what if there really IS a tabby cat called Fancy Pants somewhere in Lime Bay?" Evie said. "Because if there is—"

"Then Agent B will deliver him straight to the diner." Iris burst out laughing. "Your stepmom is going to go nuts!"

"Wait—why would she take your cat to some diner?" Zak asked.

"Oh yeah, sorry," Evie said. "I keep forgetting you don't know. I moved here three weeks ago, and my stepmom and dad own the diner opposite the boardwalk."

Iris made a face at her cousin. "If you ever left the bookstore, you'd know all that."

"Hey, Fudge is barking," Evie said before Zak could reply. "Come on, let's go check on him."

They dashed across the yard, dodging an angry goat that was headbutting Gammy as she tried to put it back in its pen, while Dawn rounded up the last of the escaped dogs.

But as they got closer, Evie could see Fudge didn't look like himself. His ears were down. His tail was droopy, and he was tugging on his leash to try to break free. "Hey, little guy, what's the matter?" Evie bent down to snuggle him, and the pup jumped into her lap and tried to hide his head under her arm. "Aw, look, he's shivering."

"No wonder," Iris said, crouching down next to them. "This place is like a jungle."

"Yep, another major mess-up by the Agents of H.E.A.R.T.!" Zak added, squatting down on the other side of Evie.

"But this wasn't really Agent B's fault." Evie tickled Fudge's ears, and his tail began to wag again. "She was just trying to help. And she did give me Fudge . . ."

"I suppose," Iris said. "But the other two agents are useless."

"I don't know . . . ," Evie said. "If Agent C hadn't turned Fudge into a donkey, then I wouldn't have crashed into the twins and come up with my Sandcastle Sundaes idea . . ." Zak looked at her blankly, but she carried on. "And Agent R . . . well, she really thinks I'm going to be locked in a tower, so she's doing everything she can to make sure I can escape."

"That's not going to happen," Iris said.

"Yeah, but she thinks it is," Evie said, stroking Fudge's ears so his tail wagged even more. "So it's kind of nice of her to worry."

"It is?" Iris scratched her head. "I didn't think about it like that."

"I just need to find a way to make the agents more helpful," Evie said. "It's like at the diner. My stepmom only gives me dull jobs like folding napkins and counting saucepots, when she should really be asking me to waitress and make amazing desserts. Because I'm good at those things. I mean, I know I drop stuff, but the customers like me, and they love my ice creams. And if only my stepmom could see that, she'd let me help out more—especially today, when we have the judges from the Best Café Contest coming."

"I guess the agents are just like your stepmom," Iris said. "They don't listen."

"What about the book of fairy tales?" Evie said. "Isn't there anything in there that tells you how to make the agents pay attention? Like a guide on how to use it?"

"Nah, it's just stories and pictures," Zak said. "I checked when I was trying to get rid of the agents."

Iris giggled. "I keep thinking about your wish, Zak, and how the agents thought you wanted a *spouse* instead of a *mouse*! That's hilarious."

Zak's face turned red. "Not as funny as you turning up to ball practice in a frilly frock!"

Evie suddenly thought about her own wish. She remembered being mad at her parents and asking if she could be more involved in the diner and then—"Wait!" she blurted out. "That's the problem! The agents always get the wish a little wrong."

Iris and Zak looked at her.

"See, I've remembered exactly what I wished for," Evie said. "I told my parents I wanted to help out in the diner more. And if they wouldn't let me, then I wished I could go home, back to my old house. But of course, I didn't really want that . . . I wanted to work in the diner."

"Yep, that's exactly why I dumped the book," Iris said. "Because the agents NEVER listen and even when they do, they don't fix things in a useful way."

"Maybe it's because they don't understand what we really need," Evie said. "See, they only have their own stories to go by. So Agent R is always trying to keep people out of towers—because she got stuck in one. Agent C thinks a bit of magic and a pumpkin coach will solve every problem, because it made her life better—"

"And beasts are what makes Agent B happy," Iris interrupted. "So, she believes it must be the same for everyone else."

"I agree about the beasts," Zak said, tickling Fudge's ears again. "I'd love a pet."

"Me too," Evie said. "But that doesn't help me with my wish to help out in the diner. Like I told you, today is the Best Café Contest. And I REALLY want to help my parents win. I even invented this awesome dessert for it, called Sandcastle Sundaes," she added for Zak's benefit. "But I probably won't get a chance to show the judges. Unless—" Evie's eyes suddenly sparkled. "Unless, the agents could fix that somehow and make me into the best wait-ress ever, so I could prove to my stepmom how great my desserts are, AND help her win the contest, and then she'll want me to be more involved in the diner in the future—and let me keep Fudge!"

Iris snorted. "I'm not sure even the Agents of H.E.A.R.T. could do that."

"Why not?" Evie jumped up. "Come on. Let's get

back to the diner. I'm sure if I got the chance to explain it to the agents—*really* make them understand, then they could help me!"

"Nah, it won't work," Iris said. "They still won't listen!"

Zak tapped his chin with his finger for a moment. "Mmm, I think I know how Evie could get them to pay attention. Give me half an hour. I'll meet you back at the diner." And he dashed out the shelter gate.

CHAPTER 17

"Oh, that goat!" Gammy came striding over, her dress covered in fluff and her hat slightly chewed. "She'll eat anything!"

Iris and Evie tried not to laugh.

"Where's Zak?" Gammy asked.

"Um, he said he had to go fetch something," Iris said. "He's meeting us back at the diner."

"Oh, okay." Gammy nodded. "Now, I'm afraid I've got some bad news." She looked at Evie. "I'm sorry, but Dawn can't take Fudge today—not while she's still trying to settle the animals down after the chaos in here."

Evie tried not to look too excited. "Oh, er . . . that's a shame. I guess I'll just take Fudge back to the diner, then. I'm sure Hannah won't mind." She felt her cheeks redden at the fib she'd just told.

"I think we'd all better get going," Gammy said. "Your stepmom will be worried."

Outside, Evie felt as light as a cloud as they headed back down to the main street. *Not only do I STILL have you,* she smiled down at Fudge, *I've also got THE best plan to fix everything. The agents are going to turn me into a real Wonder Waitress, and then I'm going to serve the judge my Sandcastle Sundae and we'll win the award for sure, and then Hannah will be so happy she'll let me keep you forever . . .*

But as they turned the corner, Iris suddenly grabbed her arm. "Look!" she gasped, pointing to a chalkboard outside the Pembertons' café.

Evie glanced at the board, which was advertising

the café's daily specials. She read down the list . . . *Chocolate Whip, Blackberry Smoothie, Pineapple Sorbet* . . . But as her eyes continued down, her gaze suddenly rested on one particular dessert in bigger writing than the rest. Her heart seemed to miss a beat. "No way! They wouldn't do that!"

"Ice Cream Sundae Sandcastles!" Iris read aloud. "They stole your idea."

Evie felt a tidal wave of anger wash up from her belly. *How could they? Of all the rotten, dirty tricks . . .*

Just then the café door opened, and the twins appeared.

"Oh, hello," Katie-Belle said. "We saw you through the window."

"Well, she would be hard to miss with that hair." Clara giggled. "Only joking," she added with a smirk.

Evie's cheeks burned, but she still managed to stick out her chin and look them squarely in the face. "You took my idea!"

"Huh? I don't know what you're talking about," Clara replied, her face turning hard and scowly.

Evie pointed at the sign. "My ice cream idea . . . I told you about it on the beach and—"

"Nope. Don't remember that," Clara interrupted. "Do you, Katie-Belle?"

Her sister shook her head. "I do remember we had started building a giant sand palace, which you pulverized." She glared at Evie. "But luckily that was when we came up with our amazing ice cream sundae dessert. We told Mama all about it and she couldn't wait to get it on the menu, especially as today is the Best Café Contest day."

"But that's not fair," Evie said. "It was my idea."

"Yeah, you guys are liars!"

"Iris!" Gammy frowned. "That's not a nice word. Perhaps the girls just thought of it at the same time. That sometimes happens. Don't worry, Evie, I'm sure you've got loads of other brilliant ideas."

"But Gammy, they DID steal it—" Iris began.

"Come on!" Gammy had already started

walking away. "Evie's stepmom will be worrying about her."

The girls reluctantly followed. But behind them, Evie could hear the twins giggling. Then one said in a loud voice: "I hope the judge likes our new dessert. We're certain to win now."

Evie bit her lip. *If only I hadn't told them my idea! What with their fancy café AND my Sandcastle Sundaes, there's no way they won't win the contest.* She felt her eyes prickle. *Don't cry, Wonder Waitress!* she told herself. But for some reason her eyes didn't seem to be listening. Fudge nuzzled at her ankles as though he knew she was sad. She reached down and tickled his ears, her eyes blurry with tears. *Oh, Fudge, how will I convince Hannah to let me keep you if I can't even help her win the contest? Everything had to be perfect and now it's just a giant mess.*

As they drew level with Gammy's flower stall, an older man in yellow pants and a floppy cap, who was standing there, waved to them.

"Oh, there's Bryan," Gammy said. "I'd better go see how he's doing. Are you girls going into the diner?"

Evie nodded.

"Okay, I'll catch up with you later."

"You all right?" Iris whispered to Evie when Gammy had gone. "The twins are so mean."

Evie wiped her hand across her eyes. "I'm fine, but I'm crankier than a croc with a toothache! I can't believe they stole my idea." She gritted her teeth and stood up straighter. "But I'm not going to let them beat me."

"Have you got any other desserts that could smash them?" Iris asked.

Evie tugged at the scratchy braid and thought for a moment. "Well, there was this one I invented last night when Dad was baking. I made a whole tub of it. It's in the freezer. You could try some if you like. I called it Toffee-Topper-Space-Hopper. And it's got blue moon ice cream in it, and popping candy and mini meringues and toffee sauce and—"

"Er, that sounds super yummy," Iris interrupted. "Only, the name . . . what was it again? Toffee-hopper-flopper-bottle-stopper-deelie-bopper? It's kind of . . . um . . . lumpy?" She smiled her wide, gap-toothed smile and Evie couldn't help but grin back.

"Yeah, you're right." Evie sighed. "It is a bit of a mouthful. The sandcastles idea was WAY better."

"Don't worry, maybe the Agents of H.E.A.R.T. will help you come up with something else." Iris glanced around the beach. "Only I'm not sure where they've gone. They're usually hanging around . . ."

"I guess they're like buses," Evie said. "When you DON'T need one there are loads, but when you DO want one, they never seem to appear—oh, wait, there's Hannah— Hey, Han, I'm back now!" She waved to her stepmom who had appeared on the café terrace, carrying a tray of coffee cups.

Hannah waved back, then spotted Fudge and her smile vanished. "Why is that dog back here again?"

Evie was about to explain, when a customer walked past her—a man in a smart suit with a clipboard and pen in his hand. Hannah was looking at him closely. Evie watched him, too. He climbed the steps to the café's terrace, stopping at the top to look around and make a few notes, before going inside. Hannah quickly followed him into the diner.

"Oh my goodness!" Evie said. "Do you think that could be the judge?"

Iris nodded. "He looked official."

"Quick!" Evie said. "I've got to get in there and help my parents win. Even if the agents aren't here, I can still serve the judge some of the ice cream I made last night. I just need to think of a way to sneak past Hannah. Come on . . . There's a gate around the side of the diner. Follow me."

CHAPTER 18

But as they headed around the back—

"Hey, you guys. Wait up!"

Evie and Iris turned to see Zak jogging up the street toward them. His face was red, and his legs were covered in dirt. In his arms was a cardboard box. "I found it!" he puffed. "This will make the agents listen."

"Are you okay?" Iris asked. "You looked kind of—"

"Bedraggled!" Evie smiled. It was a word her dad had used when they'd camped out last summer and got caught in a rainstorm.

Zak collapsed against the wall of the café, panting and trying to get his words out. "They came looking for you, by the way," he gasped. "At the b-b-bookstore!"

"Who?" Evie frowned. "Not the twins?"

"No, two of the Agents of H.E.A.R.T.—Agent C and Agent R!" He paused for a moment to catch his breath. "I had to sneak out the cellar window so they wouldn't see me." He put the box in Evie's hands. "Open it!"

"What is it?" Evie asked, pulling back the flaps at the top and peeping inside.

"Here, let me show you." Zak lifted out a square black box about the size of a lunch box, with little knobs and dials down one side.

"A radio?" Evie said.

"It's the mini amp!" Iris cried, suddenly looking interested. "I used this last year at the festival when

I played my guitar—there should be a pin micro-phone in there, too," she added, leaning in to look in the box.

"Yep, I've got it." Zak dangled a wire in front of him with a little squishy microphone on one end.

"But I don't play guitar," Evie said.

"It's not just for instruments," Zak said. "You can use it for anything where you need a loud voice."

"Neat idea!" Evie held the microphone in front of her, while Zak connected the other end into the amp and switched it on.

"Go ahead, try it," he said.

"Um . . . sure." Evie frowned. "But I don't know WHAT TO SAY—WHOA! I'M SO LOUD!"

At the sound of her booming voice, Fudge dived behind her legs.

"WAY TOO LOUD!" Iris flicked the off switch. "This is actually quite a good plan, even if it is your idea, Zak."

He gave a mock bow. "Thank you."

Evie felt a buzz of excitement in her tummy.

"There's no way the agents can ignore me with a microphone—even if they're shouting at each other, I'll still be louder than them!" She reached down and stroked Fudge. "Don't worry, boy, if they really can turn me into Wonder Waitress, I'll win this contest and be able to keep you forever!" She looked at Iris and Zak. "You do think this will work, right?"

"We're about to find out," Zak said. "Look!"

Running down the street, their frilly frocks flapping, their fabulous hairdos bouncing in the breeze, came the three agents.

"Quick, turn on the amp!" Zak said.

"Not here. We've got to get into the yard first." Evie led the way through the gate. But Iris hung back.

"I'll try to slow them down," she called. "Shout when you're ready."

In the backyard, Zak pointed to the trampoline. "Stand on that; it'll make you taller than them. Mom always stands on a box when she introduces speakers at the bookstore."

Evie tied Fudge's leash to the trampoline, then clambered up on top. Zak placed the amp at her feet and handed her the mic to attach to her shirt. Her hands were shaking as she put it on. *I just hope this works; otherwise in about five minutes, I could find myself stuck in another potato cart, heading nowhere!*

"Ready?" Zak asked.

Evie hesitated. Her tummy felt full of butterflies. *No, not butterflies, more like a giant flock of parakeets doing a whole bunch of loop-de-loops!* She took a deep breath and nodded.

CHAPTER 19

Agent C was first through the gate, still limping with only one shoe. "Evie! There you are! Guess what I found at the bookstore?" She waggled a thin pamphlet in the air. "A guide to magic wands!"

Zak, who was now hiding behind one of the yard chairs, looked across at Evie with wide eyes and shrugged.

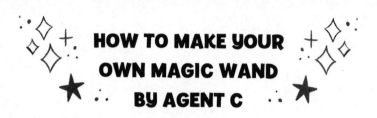

HOW TO MAKE YOUR OWN MAGIC WAND BY AGENT C

According to Agent C, every princess needs a magic wand. And this is her guide on how to make one. Don't forget to make up your own magic words, too. Agent C says her spells work better when she makes them rhyme.

You will need:

- A short, sturdy twig

- Crafting materials such as scraps of fabric, ribbons, pipe cleaners, colored/shiny paper, beads, stickers, paints, and shells

- Or natural materials like feathers, leaves, flowers, pine cones, etc.

- Glue or rubber bands

Method:

- Make sure your twig is dry before beginning.

- Plan your wand design. Draw it out on paper, or lay out your materials in the style you wish to apply them.

- Consider a theme for your wand: glitter sparkles, winter snowflakes, hearts, woodland, pets, sports spells, mermaids, or pumpkins!

- Attach, wrap, or glue all your materials to your stick. (A glue gun works best if you have one, but ensure that an adult helps with this as they can be very hot and dangerous!)

- If you don't have glue, you can tie your materials onto your wand or secure with elastic bands.

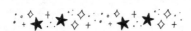

"Isn't it wonderful!" Agent C beamed at Evie. "With this guide, the magic wand will do exactly what we want. And look what else I found . . ." She held up a slightly squishy, bashed-up pumpkin. "Would you believe someone actually put this in the trash? Now we'll have a proper coach to transport you home." Before Evie could reply, Agent B skipped through the gate. "Evie, my pet, I found him. Fancy Pants is back!"

Evie blinked at the small tabby cat, sitting on Agent B's shoulder, peeping out from under her big hair.

"Though it's a bit strange," Agent B said, reaching up to tickle the kitty. "He keeps telling me he lives on the other side of town, behind a trash can, not here at the diner . . ." She stroked his head. "Or perhaps I'm just misunderstanding him. Cat language is much harder than dog!"

Or maybe he really DOES live on the other side of town, Evie thought, *and he's wondering why you've brought him here.*

The cat suddenly caught sight of Fudge and let out a loud hiss.

"Oh, no, no," Agent B soothed. "You must be friends! You're both Evie's protector beasts!"

But Fudge didn't seem to want to be friends. He shuffled backward under the trampoline, straining at his leash, and hid behind a beach ball that was stuck there.

"Hey, Evie!" Agent R shouted, as she jogged through the gate a moment later. "I've got the tiara!"

Iris, who had followed her into the yard, was looking goggle-eyed at the sparkly hairpiece Agent R was waving in the air. "I can't believe you actually found one," Iris muttered.

And that's not the only shock, Evie thought, looking at Agent B and the cat on her shoulder.

"Huh?" Iris did a double take when she saw it. "Oh, my giddy aunt—first the tiara and now she's found a Fancy Pants!"

Agent R snorted. "Well, I don't know why you're

so shocked about the tiara. I went to the store you told me about. Though it was WAY farther than you said."

Iris glanced at Evie, her eyes so wide with shock that such a store actually existed—not to mention that there really was a cat called Fancy Pants— Evie nearly burst out laughing. Suddenly she didn't feel nervous anymore . . . "HELLO, AGENTS OF H.E.A.R.T.!" she said, startling even herself with how loud she sounded, thanks to the microphone.

The agents jumped, too.

"PLEASE LISTEN!" she boomed. "I AM GRATE- FUL FOR YOUR HELP, BUT I NEED YOU TO PAY ATTENTION TO WHAT I AM ABOUT TO SAY."

The agents were so surprised to be yelled at, they all fell silent and gazed at Evie, each of their mouths open in a perfect O.

"WHEN I MADE MY WISH," Evie bellowed, "YOU ONLY HEARD THE SECOND PART. BUT I NEED YOUR HELP WITH THE FIRST BIT, SO I'M GOING TO SAY MY WISH AGAIN, MUCH MORE CLEARLY."

She glanced at Iris, who gave her a thumbs-up. "I WISH THAT I COULD BE A WAITRESS IN MY PARENTS' DINER! UM, THAT'S IT." She decided not to bother mentioning the other part about going home again, if she couldn't be a waitress, just in case it caused confusion.

The agents stared at Evie for one long moment, then—

"Why didn't you say so?" Agent R said. "It would have saved a lot of time."

"Perhaps Fancy Pants could help, too?" Agent B suggested. "I've been to loads of cat cafés where customers can cuddle the pets, and they're *paw-sitively purr-fect*!"

"Stand back, everyone!" Agent C said, pushing past the other two agents. "I am the expert in catering. Did I ever tell you about my stepmom and stepsisters?"

"Just a thousand times," Agent R muttered.

Agent C's nostrils flared but she carried on: "I've fetched and carried and cooked and cleaned and cared for my stepfamily so much, I could write a book about it."

You kind of already have, what with the fairy tales book and all, Evie thought.

"You'll need an apron!" Agent C said. "Something bright and cheerful. Then there are those sandals," she added, looking at Evie's footwear. "They'll never do! Now, I just need to check my handbook for the right spell . . ." While she began leafing through the pages, Agent R shouldered her out of the way.

"So, you want to be a waitress, do ya?" She peered at Evie's head. "Well, that braid has got to go. It'll trip you up! If you're serving any wicked witches, you're bound to spill their smoothies and wicked witches HATE spilled smoothies. That's why I ended up in a tower."

Huh? Evie and Iris exchanged glances. *Rapunzel? A waitress? Whoa!* That definitely wasn't what happened in the version they'd read.

"Yep, we'll chop the braid off!" Agent R said.

Evie's eyes brightened. Cutting off the hairpiece was the best thing she'd heard all day. "Yes, please!" she said. Then she stopped. *Huh?* Her voice sounded kind of quiet again. She glanced down at the amp. "Uh-oh! The light's gone off."

Iris darted forward. "Is it broken? Hey—quit hiding, Zak! Come help me fix this thing. Evie needs her loud voice, or they're going to take over again."

But it was too late, the agents weren't listening to anyone but themselves now. And suddenly, three super-shiny, bright-eyed, over-eager fairy-tale faces turned on Evie like sharks at a sardine buffet.

"It's time to get started!" Agent R said. "This is going to be fun!"

CHAPTER 20

Agent C was first to pounce. She poked Rapunzel out of the way with her magic wand. "I'm going to make you into the best waitress ever. But first you'll need a snazzy outfit."

Uh-oh! Hope this doesn't hurt. Evie closed her eyes and a puff of purple smoke enveloped her. She shivered. *Oooh, this feels weird. Sort of hot and cold and tingly, like being under a water hose on a sunny day—huh?* She opened her eyes and found her blue shorts and shirt had vanished, and she was now wearing a glowing pink dress with an orange apron that sparkled in the sunshine.

"Wow!" Iris breathed. "The diners are going to need sunglasses."

"It makes my eyes hurt." Zak, who had crept out from behind his chair to try to fix the amp, made a pained face.

"Try spinning around," Agent C said, her eyes twinkling.

Nervously, Evie did a twirl and tiny bubbles popped out of the apron as she moved. "Wow—that IS kind of neat!"

"You don't need bubbles," Agent R said, shoulder barging Agent C out of the way. "What you need is a mega-blaster makeover. Stand by for a total transformation." And she unzipped her belt bag.

Evie glanced down at Zak, who was still fiddling with the amp. "Did you fix it yet?" she whispered. "Because I really don't think they're going to listen to me without it."

"Um, it could be the batteries," Zak said.

"Take them out and give them a rub," Iris suggested. "That's what Gammy does when the TV remote stops working. Oooh, look at that!" she added, as Agent R took out a spray can and gave it a squirt. "It's turned the grass bright orange."

Evie felt her tummy flip-flop. *I DON'T want THAT on my hair!*

Agent C let out a happy squeal. "I've had another idea. We'll make you a tasting plate. A little tray of nibbles to tempt your diners. And I know exactly what we can serve—my fairy godmother's favorite dessert: pumpkin sorbet!"

Zak wrinkled his nose. "Sounds *bleurgh!*"

"And we can use this to make it!" Agent C held up the rotten pumpkin.

Evie grimaced. Rotten-pumpkin sorbet did not sound like an award-winning dish. "Er, if you don't mind, I'D RATHER USE MY OWN ICE CREAM! OH!" she boomed. "THE MICROPHONE IS WORK-ING AGAIN!"

"Not for long," Zak muttered. "See, the light keeps flashing on and off."

Agent C did a little leap in the air. "Oh wow, Evie, your very own ice cream? What a marvelous plan!" She fist-pumped the air a few times. "Where is this dessert you've made?"

"IT'S IN A GREEN TUB IN THE BIG FREEZER IN THE KITCHEN."

"I'll fetch it," Beauty said. "Come on, Fancy Pants, let's get you back into your cozy café home."

"NO WAIT—" Evie blasted. "CATS AREN'T allowed in the—" But just then the microphone cut out again. "Stop!" she shouted to Beauty. But Agent B didn't stop. *Oh no! If my parents see a cat in the diner, they'll flip. I've got to go after her.* She unclipped the microphone and dived off the trampoline, and straight into the path of Agent R.

CHAPTER 21

"Time for your makeover," Agent R said, holding up her hairdressing scissors and comb.

"But I've got to stop Beauty—" Evie began.

SNIP! Agent R had already lopped off half the braid.

"Oooh." Evie waggled her neck from side to side. "That feels so much better; light and free and—ow! That tugs!"

Agent R was now wildly back combing what was

left of the braid high into the air. "Moo meed man mupdoo!" she mumbled, with her mouth full of pins, which Evie thought probably translated into "you need an updo."

"Make sure you put on loads of hair spray," Agent C said, patting her own hair, which looked as solid as a concrete slab. "We don't want your locks dangling in someone's soup."

"Does it look okay?" Evie whispered to Iris who was staring openmouthed as Agent R began squirting spray on her creation.

"Um . . . sure," Iris said. "Though it's kind of reminding me of the Empire State Building."

Zak's face bulged as he tried to contain his laughter. "I'm also seeing Marge Simpson, except with orange hair."

"Marge Simpson?" Evie squirmed around to try to look up to see what was happening on the top of her head, but Agent R just tugged the hair tighter.

"Now, just got to add the tiara . . ." Agent R plunked the sparkly hairpiece on the front, wedging it into the stiff mountain of hair. "There! What do you think?" But she wasn't asking Evie.

"Not bad," Agent C said, looking her up and down.

"Can I see?" Evie asked. "Have you got a mirror?"

Both agents gasped.

"A mirror?" Agent R said in a choked sort of a voice. "We NEVER use mirrors."

"Not ever!" Agent C said, folding her arms. "Mirrors are far too dangerous."

"They told me that, too," Iris whispered. "I think it's the whole *'mirror, mirror, on the wall, who is the fairest of them all'* thing. They're terrified of them."

Agent C was pacing up and down now, still looking at Evie. "There's something missing . . ." Then her gaze dropped to her own bare foot. "Oh, yes, shoes. What do waitresses wear on their feet?"

"Definitely NOT glass slippers!" Agent R said with a snort.

Agent C stared at Evie's feet for a moment, then smiled. "Oh, I know exactly what you need."

"You do?" Evie gulped. *Why don't I like the sound of this . . . ?*

"Rocket boots!" Agent C squealed. "You'll be the fastest waitress in the world!"

Evie's eyes goggled. "B-b-but I can't wear rocket boots."

Too late!

With one tap of Agent C's wand, Evie's sandals had vanished and in their place were a pair of silver roller skates with blaster rockets at the back.

Zak whistled. "Now, *those* are cool."

Evie couldn't stop staring at them. They were bigger and shinier than her own roller skates, with lightning flashes down the side, and huge silver wheels on the bottom. "Whoa!" She grabbed hold of the edge of the trampoline to stop herself falling. "So slippery! And my feet feel kind of warm and—"

"Oh, that's probably just their engines heating up," Agent C interrupted. "You're going to be able to get so much more done with these on. If only

I'd had a pair when I was running around looking after my stepmom and stepsisters."

"I really don't think—" Evie began. But she was drowned out by a roaring sound from her heels, and the boots began to shudder.

"Ready?" Agent C asked.

"Definitely not!" Evie clung to the side of the trampoline. "Look, I love my outfit. And I'm sure my hair is nice . . ." She glanced at Agent R who puffed out her chest proudly. "But I can't wear rocket boots in the diner. See, there's a judge in there right now, and if he sees me waitressing with these things on my feet, there's no way we'll win the competition, and then my parents will be sad and I'll be sad, too, because I'm trying to make them see how useful I

can be so that they'll let me help more and spend time with them AND maybe even let me keep Fudge and—hey, you're not listening, are you?"

Agent C was doing some strange stretches now, standing on tiptoe, with her hands above her head. And then suddenly she shouted: "Give me an *H*!" And she moved her arms into a shape that sort of looked like an *H*.

Agent R rolled her eyes. "Not this again."

"Give me an *E*," Agent C yelled, making another outline with her arms and legs that did not look at all like an *E*. "Give me an *A*, an *R*, and a big, big *T*," she went on, bending her body into ever more awkward movements. "And what will you beeeeee? Happily Ever After!"

"That is so lame," Zak muttered. "It doesn't even rhyme."

"I keep telling her it sucks," Agent R said. "Hey, Cinders! What about the ice cream?"

"Oh yes, I forgot." Agent C stopped posing for a moment and cupped her hands around her mouth. "BEAUTY!" she hollered. "We need that dessert!"

"Quick!" Evie whispered to Iris and Zak. "Help me get these boots off. If I let go of the trampoline, I think they'll carry me away."

But just then the kitchen door burst open and Beauty—WITHOUT the cat—came jogging up the path with a tray in her arms. "I've got the ice cream!"

"Um, where's Fancy Pants?" Evie called. But none of the agents were listening. "Good work," Agent C said to Beauty.

"Yes, and I've just had a *feather-tastic* idea on how to serve it!" Beauty gave a long, low whistle, and the air was instantly filled with the sound of wings fluttering, as a dozen or so tiny sparrows flew down and landed on the tray in her arms. She bent her head and began to chirrup to them.

"What's she doing?" Evie whispered.

"Showing off!" Agent R muttered.

Then—POP! The birds vanished, and in their place were tiny bird-shaped ceramic dishes.

"So cute!" Agent C said.

Evie's eyes nearly fell out. "How on earth—"

"Oh, birds are terribly clever," Agent B said. "They can magically morph themselves into anything they like! And, lucky you, Evie, they agreed to turn themselves into tiny little tasting bowls for you to serve your ice cream to your customers. But only for half an hour. So let's dish up and get you inside."

"I'll help!" Agent C said. And with one sweep of her wand the tub of ice cream vanished, and the bird bowls were filled with ice cream. The tray had changed, too, sparkling and glittering as though it were made of diamonds.

"Here!" Beauty said, holding it out to Evie.

Without thinking, Evie reached to take it. But as soon as she let go of the trampoline, her feet began to move forward. "Whoa!" She wobbled wildly, trying not to let the tray fall. "The boots have got a mind of their own."

Agent C's eyes twinkled. "That's because I put a waitressing spell on them. They'll take you straight to the diner. And then they'll only work if you're carrying your tray and serving people. Enjoy your *Happily Ever After*, Evie! Goodbye, goodbye, now."

"No—stop! I can't waitress in rocket boots." But suddenly, with a loud roar of engines, flames shot out of the heels and the boots began to whizz toward the diner. Fudge dived out from under the trampoline, tugging his leash free, and chased after her. "No, no, Fudge, you can't come with me," Evie called, trying not to turn around to look at him in case she lost her balance entirely.

"Don't worry, I've got him," Zak called, grabbing his leash.

The pup let out a howl of dismay at not being able to follow Evie.

"I'm so sorry, Fudge," she called. "I won't be long." *Fingers crossed!* Then she disappeared through the kitchen door.

CHAPTER 22

"Ahhh!" Evie bent her knees and tried to keep her balance as she zoomed into the kitchen—a cloud of bubbles flying out from her apron. "Help! Oh, I mean—hi!" She waved as she passed her dad, who was ladling soup into bowls.

"What on earth?" Her dad froze, his mouth open, his eyes wide. He dropped the spoon he was holding. But by the time he was able to get some more words out, Evie had already passed into the diner.

"Hey, Hannah!" Evie tried not to catch her step-mom's eye as she appeared through the doorway. *Maybe no one will notice me,* she told herself. *And I can just do a quick spin around the dining room and then zip right back out to the yard.*

But there was no way Hannah had failed to see her . . .

"Evie? What on earth?" Her stepmom's eyes were as round as dinner plates. She looked at Evie's hair, her clothes, and then at her boots. "W-w-what are you doing?" she spluttered. "The judge is here."

"Don't worry," Evie said, feeling her stomach begin to churn on full super-fast-food-mixer mode. "I think I've got the rocket boots under control now. See, I'm going to stop right here—" She tried to grab the counter as she passed it, but her feet kept mov-ing. "It's okay," she called back to her stepmom. "The boots are slowing down now." *Yep, definitely slower, and less noisy, too, so I've no idea why everyone's staring at me . . .* Then she remembered how freaky she must look with her crazy orange hair and sparkly apron, not to mention the bubbles that were now swirling around the room.

Conversation had stopped dead in the diner the moment Evie had blasted through the doorway. Every head had turned. Every face was fixed on her. The silence was—

Deafening!

Say something, Wonder Waitress, she told herself as she glided into the middle of the tables, trying to ignore all the looks she was getting. But what could she say? What could possibly explain what they were seeing? But then—*I've got it! Pretend this is normal. Act as if there's nothing unusual about a waitress wearing rocket boots.* Evie forced the biggest smile onto her face. "Hey, everyone!" she said, holding out the tray of bird-shaped bowls to the nearest table. "Want to try some of our latest dessert? It's, um . . . out of this world!" The boots had slowed now, the heels emitting a gentle chug as they hovered next to the table.

"Oooh," breathed the little girl who was sitting there with her mom and baby brother. "I love your tiara."

"You do? Um, thanks. Would you like to try it on?" Evie tugged it out of her solid hairdo and handed it to the girl. "And have some ice cream, too," she added, laying two bowls on the table.

"Look, Mommy," the little girl said, putting the tiara on her own head.

"Very pretty." Her mom smiled at Evie. "Thanks, that's so kind of you."

"Bubbles!" the little girl cried, as a shower of them popped out of Evie's apron.

Evie wafted more bubbles in the little girl's direction, as the boots moved her slowly on to the next table. *Wow, that's weird; now that I'm waitressing, the boots don't seem so wobbly.*

"Hi, how are you doing?" she said, trying not to look at the faces of the older couple whose table she'd now arrived at. They were frozen like statues, their sandwiches held halfway between their mouths and their plates, as they stared at her in disbelief. "I hope you're enjoying your meal. Please try our new dessert . . . Hello there," she added to the people at the next table, while the boots continued their journey around the room. "Do you want to try our super-cool new ice cream?"

And on and on she went. Evie trundled around the tables, delivering ice cream and bubbles to the shocked diners, while Hannah—and her dad, who Evie could see had appeared from the kitchen—just stared in horror, wringing their hands and glancing at the customers to see their reaction.

But after a few moments the shock of Evie's unusual entrance seemed to pass, and the diners began to chat and laugh and smile at one another again.

This is actually going okay . . . Evie looked around

the room and noticed people were enjoying themselves. *And they love the ice cream!* she thought as she saw lots of them digging in.

"Pardon me," said a small voice behind her. "Here's your tiara."

Evie turned to find the little girl behind her. "Oh, that's okay. You can keep it. I've got another one upstairs. Would you like some more ice cream?"

"Yes, please," the little girl said. "It's sooo yummy."

Evie felt a warm tingly feeling in her tummy as she handed the ice cream to the girl.

"I like the popping candy best," the little girl said. "It makes my mouth all fizzy-whizzy!" She giggled and ran back to her mom.

Through the windows of the diner, Evie saw Iris and Zak had appeared on the front terrace with Fudge. She gave them a thumbs-up and they smiled back. But when she reached the final table in the room, Evie's heart seemed to miss a beat and her legs turned to jelly. *It's him: the judge guy!*

It was the man she'd seen earlier, with the smart

suit and the clipboard. He had a stern look on his face and his fingers were tapping on the table. The clipboard lay in front of him and Evie could see lots of words scribbled and underlined in black pen.

Evie took a deep breath. "Um . . . hi," she said, her throat suddenly drier than the Sahara. "Would you like to try our new ice cream?"

"No, thank you." The man blinked at her like he had flies in his eyes. "I don't like dessert." He tried to waft away a cloud of bubbles that had drifted across the table, but they were already popping and turning into damp circles on the arm of his smart suit.

"Oh, let me wipe that for you." Evie picked up the corner of her apron to dab at the bubble patches. But as she reached over, she felt something furry brush past her legs. She glanced down. The man did, too . . .

"A cat!" he cried, jerking his chair back from the table as Fancy Pants jumped onto the chair next to him.

"Oh no! He really shouldn't be here," Evie said. "But please don't worry—I'm sure he's friendly."

The man gazed in horror at the cat and pushed his chair even farther away from it.

"Don't you like cats?" Evie said. "I read this book once, and it said cats can tell who likes them and who doesn't, and they always seem to go to the people who don't like them, which is weird, but—"

"Ahhh!" the man screamed as the cat suddenly jumped from its seat onto his lap.

But thankfully the noise of his hollering was drowned out by a sudden THWUMP as the front door of the diner burst open and a little hairy lump scrambled inside and threw itself at Evie.

CHAPTER 23

"Fudge!" Evie dropped her tray on the judge's table and scooped up the wriggly pup and buried her face in his furry neck. "Were you missing me too much?" For a second or two, she just stood there hugging him and breathing in his warm doggy smell. Then—

"This is outrageous!" the man snapped, standing up and tipping Fancy Pants off his knee. "Dogs AND cats are not permitted in diners!"

Evie's eyes popped open. She looked at the customer's horrified face and felt her tummy drop into her toes. *Uh-oh! This is definitely a 10 on the Scale of Super-Cranky Customer Meltdowns.* "I am so sorry," Evie said, trying to stop the pup from leaning over and licking the man's face. "Fudge hasn't quite got the hang of the rules yet. He doesn't realize he's a dog and he's not allowed in here. But I'm going to take him outside now." Evie tried to skate to the door, but the boots wouldn't budge. *Huh?* She tried again, but still nothing happened. For a second, she considered telling the man the truth: that her boots were enchanted waitressing footwear and they only worked if the wearer was serving customers. Instead she waved to Iris and Zak through the window. "Help!" she mouthed.

In a second, they were through the door. Fancy Pants shot through their legs and out onto the terrace, while Zak scooped up Fudge and he and Iris dashed back outside. But it was too late.

"Check!" the man called, waving to Hannah.

"Please, won't you try the ice cream?" Evie said, her hands shaking as she picked up the tray and held it out to him. "I'm sure you'd love it, if you could just give it a chance."

The man shook his head. "I don't like dessert! And I HATE dogs! And cats! And—and—everything about this café!" He grabbed his clipboard and stomped off to the counter.

Evie's shoulders slumped and her head hung low. She picked up her tray and the boots began to move again. She tried not to look at her step-mom, who was dealing with the cranky judge man. *What's Hannah going to say? I've completely ruined our chances of winning the contest. She'll never let me help in the diner now or keep Fudge . . .*

But as she drew level with the table where the little girl was sitting with her mom and baby brother, Evie realized they were waving to her.

"Hi, can I get you something?" Evie asked. "And I am SO sorry about the animals."

The mom smiled. "Don't worry. I thought you

handled the situation very well. You were calm and kind and so polite to that customer."

"I was?"

"Sure. In fact, I was just making some notes about how well you coped with the unexpected cat and dog visitors, in my review." The lady pointed to a small notebook on the table in front of her. "I also wanted to let you know that Amber and I LOVED your dessert."

The little girl giggled. "I love the tiara, too."

"And your outfit and your hair! And those bubbles." The lady whistled. "Wow! It's all so much fun! It's really like nothing I've ever seen before."

Evie felt her face flush. She smiled and looked at her boots. "Um, thanks."

"Which is why I have decided to award you— and your diner—the Golden Coffee Cup Award for Best Café in Lime Bay. Congratulations!" And she held out a rosette to Evie.

"Excuse me?" Evie wondered if she was seeing things. "I don't understand . . . I mean . . ." She

paused for a second, processing everything the lady had just said. "Are you the judge? But I thought he was the—" Evie glanced back to the counter where the man in the suit had finished paying his check and was now filling in a customer feedback card.

The lady giggled. "Well, I guess you can't please everyone," she whispered. "But you certainly made us happy. I always bring my children with me when I'm reviewing cafés. I think the way a diner welcomes families is one of the most important skills to test. And you made Amber feel very special. In fact, that's one of the other things I love about this place. There's a real family atmosphere."

The little girl beamed up at Evie. "We're going to come every day, aren't we, Mommy?"

"Well, I don't know about every day." The lady chuckled. "But we'll definitely be back. Oh, and just one more thing . . . What do you call that delicious dessert that you were handing out?"

Evie glanced outside to the terrace, where Iris and Zak were waiting for her with Fudge. Then she gazed around at all the empty dessert bowls on the tables, and the happy customers chatting and smiling at one another, and finally she took a deep breath and forced herself to look across to her parents who were staring in astonishment at the rosette Evie was holding. And suddenly she knew exactly what to name the dessert. "It's called *Happily Ever After* Ice Cream," she said, and for a moment she thought she might pop with the warm bubble of joy that seemed to be filling her chest.

EVIE BROWN'S HAPPILY EVER AFTER ICE CREAM

A sweet and tasty treat for special occasions!

You will need:

- Blue moon ice cream—store-bought or homemade

- Mini marshmallows

- Toffee/chocolate sauce

- Mini meringues

- Popping candy

Ingredients for homemade blue moon ice cream:

- ½ cup and five tablespoons sweetened condensed milk

- 2½ cups double cream/heavy whipping cream

- 1 teaspoon of vanilla extract

- 1 teaspoon of raspberry essence (optional)

- 1 teaspoon of lemon essence (optional)

- A handful of mini marshmallows

- A few drops of blue food coloring gel (or decorate with fresh blueberries when serving)

- Freezer-proof container (prechilled in the refrigerator ahead of making)

- Plastic wrap

Method:

- Put condensed milk, cream, vanilla, marshmallows, food coloring, and essences (if using) in an electric mixer and whisk until stiff.

- Line a prechilled freezer container with plastic wrap.

- Press mixture into container and freeze for 4-6 hours.

To serve:

- Add mini meringues, more marshmallows, toffee/chocolate sauce, and popping candy.

CHAPTER 24

A little while later, Evie and her family (and Iris, Zak, and Fudge) gathered outside on the terrace, waiting to be presented with the Golden Coffee Cup Best Café trophy. A big crowd of Lime Bay residents and visitors had come to watch, including Gammy and her friend Bryan.

"I'm so proud of you, Evie," her stepmom whispered, as the judge made a short speech to explain why she'd chosen the Browns' diner as her winner.

"Your dad and I were talking just now," Hannah said. "And we think you should be much more involved in the diner. You've got such creative ideas."

"Oh, yes, please," Evie murmured. She was smiling so much her face was beginning to hurt.

"Though, just one thing—" Hannah said, her eyes twinkling. "Maybe leave the roller skates at home next time."

Evie giggled, and Fudge, who was at her feet, wriggled even closer to her. She reached down and stroked his head. *I wonder if now is the right time to ask whether Fudge can stay? Because Hannah definitely seems to be in her "happy place."* Evie took a deep breath. "Um, I was thinking," she began. "About Fudge . . ."

Hannah's smile turned to a worried frown. "Oh, I don't know, Evie . . ."

"But the lady at the shelter said she couldn't take him today, and I don't know if it's open on weekends and—"

"That's okay," Hannah said. "He can stay until Monday."

"Really?" *That gives me two whole days to prove to you how adorable he is!* "Thanks so much!" Evie said.

But her words were drowned out by the judge who was waving for her parents to join her up front.

"And so, I'd like you all to put your hands together," the judge said, "and congratulate Brown's Diner. "The winner of this year's Golden Coffee Cup Best Café Award!"

The crowd cheered and clapped as Evie's parents went up to accept the trophy.

Evie bent down and picked up Fudge. "I still can't believe we won," she said, snuggling the pup close.

"Neither can they!" Iris, who was standing next to her, pointed to the twins who were in the crowd watching the ceremony.

Evie felt their cranky eyes on her, and she hid her face deeper in Fudge's fluffy neck. "I don't think they'll be inviting me for a sleepover anytime soon."

Iris giggled. "Nor me! Hey—maybe we can have a sleepover together? Fudge can come, too."

"That would be awesome."

Evie wiggled her toes inside her comfy sandals. She was glad to have escaped the rocket boots. Almost as soon as the judge had given her the rosette, the boots had conked out and turned back into sandals, her hairdo had flopped, and the apron had stopped producing bubbles. The bird bowls had turned back into real birds, which had created quite a fuss in the diner, and the Agents of H.E.A.R.T. had vanished, too.

And so, it appeared, had Fancy Pants the cat. Though Iris thought she'd spotted him just before the prize giving, lurking under one of the terrace tables eating ice cream someone had dropped.

"Brown's Diner is really on the Lime Bay map now," Zak said. He was standing behind the girls, watching all the people still applauding, as Evie's parents and the judge posed for photographs.

Evie smiled. "Do you really think the agents

have gone? Forever, I mean?" She suddenly felt a little sad at the thought she might never see them again.

"I hope so," Zak said. "And I guess it makes sense. Because you got your *Happily Ever After*, right? So their work is done."

Iris snorted. "Yeah, but I wouldn't go making any crazy wishes anywhere near that book for a while, though," she said. "You never know what might happen . . ."

That night Evie slipped out of bed and fetched the fairy tales book from her shelf. Fudge, who was dozing in a box on the floor, lifted his head. His ears twitched, his tail began to thump, and he let out an excited yelp, as though he thought they might be off on another adventure somewhere.

"Shush!" Evie whispered. "Hannah said you had to be super quiet tonight, or you'll have to sleep in the woodshed."

The pup seemed to understand and quieted down, but his tail kept thumping.

Evie climbed back into bed with the book. She turned to the first story, Cinderella, and looked carefully at each page. "Look—Agent C is back in the book." She showed Fudge a picture of Cinderella at the ball. Then she checked the other stories. "They're all there, back on their pages. I guess Zak was right; the plan worked." The little cloud of disappointment she'd felt earlier descended over her once more. *I'm going to miss them. They were so fun.*

"Evie?" Hannah had appeared in the doorway. "It's time for lights off now." She came over and gently took the book from Evie's hands and laid it on the nightstand. "And you, too, Mr. Dog!" She frowned at Fudge. "I'm still not sure it was a good thing for him to stay until Monday. It might be harder for him when we take him back to the shelter."

"Do we have to?" Evie asked. "Couldn't he stay?

Please, Hannah . . . I'll give up my allowance. I'll tidy my room at least once a month. And I promise I'll never wear rocket boots again."

Her stepmom smiled. "I'm sorry, honey, but dogs aren't allowed in the diner."

"Are you still up?" Her dad appeared in the doorway. "Well done again for today, even if your outfit was a little, er, unusual!" He laughed and crossed the room to kiss her forehead. "Hannah and I are so proud of you."

"We certainly are." Hannah reached over to stroke the hair back from Evie's face. After three shampoos, most of the orange color had gone, but it still smelled of pumpkins. "That ice cream was delicious. You're definitely the best dessert chef in this family."

"Hey!" Evie's dad pretended to look offended. "That's a bit hard on the other dessert chef."

Evie giggled.

As they headed for the door, Hannah hung

back. "Oh, do you know anything about that tabby cat that appeared in the diner? It's still hanging around the kitchen door."

"Um . . ." Evie felt her cheeks grow hot.

"I kind of like it," her dad said. "I had a kitty just like it when I was a boy. And you know, every kitchen I ever worked in as a chef had a cat to keep the rodents away. And cats really can look after themselves and—"

"It's not staying!" Hannah said firmly. "Oh, and I nearly forgot, is this yours?" she added to Evie, pulling out the small glass slipper from her pocket, the one Agent C had lost earlier. "I found it in the diner and thought it must have been part of your dress-up game."

"Er, it's not actually mine," Evie said. "But I know who it belongs to."

"Oh, is it Iris's? That makes sense, because I was sure I hadn't seen it before. I'll put it here and you can give it back to her tomorrow." Hannah placed it on top of the book on Evie's nightstand and then turned off her bedside lamp. "Good night, honey," she said, closing the door behind her.

Evie shut her eyes and stretched out her toes. She thought about the strange day she'd had—about the Agents of H.E.A.R.T. and their silly ideas—and Fancy Pants, the made-up cat who turned out to be real! And about Iris and Zak, and how she'd made two great new friends in them. Then she remembered the Pemberton twins and realized she'd also made two new cranky-crocodile enemies! "And one best furry friend forever," she whispered to Fudge, through the darkness. "I just wish you could stay."

ACKNOWLEDGMENTS

Family and friends are at the center of Evie's world. And so, too, for me when writing this book.

I'd like to thank my fantastic publishing family, Feiwel and Friends, for their endless creativity, expertise, and professionalism. And especially my editor, Holly West, for guiding Evie's adventures with such skill, enthusiasm, and incredible wisdom.

Thanks also to the hugely talented Genevieve

Kote for bringing Evie and her world to life with utterly magical illustrations.

As always, I am immensely grateful to my agent Gemma Cooper, who is my book-world Fairy God-mother; she makes publishing dreams come true.

Finally, thanks to my endlessly supportive family, especially my daughter, Alice, who listened so patiently when I first imagined the H.E.A.R.T. series, and who tried and tested every recipe and activity in this book. Alice, your tiaras and magical wands were enchanting.

And to my readers, I hope you enjoy this story and that all your wishes come true.

Thank you for reading this Feiwel & Friends book.

The friends who made

HAPPILY EVER AFTER RESCUE TEAM

possible are:

Jean Feiwel, Publisher

Liz Szabla, Associate Publisher

Rich Deas, Senior Creative Director

Holly West, Senior Editor

Anna Roberto, Senior Editor

Kat Brzozowski, Senior Editor

Dawn Ryan, Executive Managing Editor

Celeste Cass, Assistant Production Manager

Erin Siu, Associate Editor

Emily Settle, Associate Editor

Foyinsi Adegbonmire, Associate Editor

Rachel Diebel, Assistant Editor

Liz Dresner, Associate Art Director

Mandy Veloso, Senior Production Editor

Follow us on Facebook or visit us online at mackids.com.

Our books are friends for life.